5⁹⁵

PELON
DROPS OUT

PELON
DROPS OUT

CELSO A. DE CASAS

2150 Shattuck Avenue
Berkeley, CA. 94704
USA
TONATIUH INTERNATIONAL INC.
PUBLISHERS OF CHICANO LITERATURE

COPYRIGHT © 1979
by CELSO A. DE CASAS

Library of Congress Catalogue Card Number: 79-84473

ISBN: 0-89229-006-4

NOTE

Cu-cui.

If you find this word in your Español/English dictionary, you have a very, very esuper edición. Hang on to it, it is valuable. The nearest equivalent to *cu-cui* in English is the bogey-man, except that the *cu-cui* is much, much worse, and scarier, too. If you don't believe this, ask Pelón. Oh yes, your bilingual diccionario will tell you that pelón means baldheaded. Pelón also means down-and-out, only more so, more down and more out.

A final word to the reader. You don't have to run to your bilingual dictionary to look up the word *syncategoremático.* It doesn't appear in this book. Now isn't that a relief?

The Editors

CONTENTS

DEDICATION

I would like to acknowledge Profesór Al Revés' role in the creation of this work. Without his unflagging enthusiasm and perseverance, neither the book nor I would be in existence. I would like to dedicate him to science so the world can know more about insanity. To Yolie, I dedicate everything, including my mustache, my pony tail and my collection of Little Jr. Chucóte records. To my mother, I dedicate "Angel Baby." I want to dedicate "You are the Sunshine of My Life" to Weempy, Mofle, Compa, Chubby, Cartoon, Feed Your Baby Donuts, Cheeks, Two-Ton Tiny, all my Homeboys at the Home for Mentally Deranged Delinquents, my aunt Monster and cousin Pickpocket, and all the cops that ever rousted me.

I dedicate "Respect" to the parents of normally looney kids. I dedicate "Time Is On My Side" to the kids of normally looney parents. I would like to dedicate "Clean Up Your Act or Lose Your Case" to all the people in trouble. To everyone needing help, I dedicate the Yellow Pages. A special dedication of "In The Still of The Night" goes out to the people patrolling the drive-in movies looking for cars with foggy windows. "I Haven't Forgotten but I Tried" goes out to the people I owe coin to. Finally, "Excuse Me One Time" goes out to my high school English teacher who said, "Never end a sentence with a preposition or you won't get over." And for sure, I can't forget Daniel, María Luz, Jofes, Lara, Rufus, Angel, Gelo, Shen, Puchi, The Boy, and Barney.

PELON DROPS OUT

What it am?

by Pelón Palomares

A lot of people pay good money for junk. Trash of all sorts is on the market. It has been said that if you promote something enough, spend a good deal of money advertising and keeping a product in front of the public's face, it will sell.

With that in mind, I sent this book to a disc jockey and bribed him with a promise of one million ears as a pledge to convince him people were listening to his show. He became very angry because the book ruined his record players and totalled-out his needles. His tape setup became hopelessly jammed when he stuck in *Pelón Drops Out* to play some choice cuts and the one million ears of corn cluttered up the radio station.

So I tried to get it on the cover of *Rolling Stone* and *Time*, figuring to get exposure among the trippy people and the people people. That didn't work so I decided to get Cheech and Chong to do a movie version of the book. No Sale. They wanted to put some dirty words in the dialogue and substitute nasties for the organic dopey stuff I take as part of my trip to other realities.

This book is meant to make people laugh, though here and there I slipped in some serious thoughts to show my philosophical talent. It is my belief that if you are going to spend good money for something, it should bring you pleasure. The price of this book should be like purchasing a ticket to enter a park or playground that offers something enjoyable at each turn of the path. The social meaning or philosophy are secondary, important only if you choose to pause along the tour. You can then sit on a rock or bench and think about what things mean, on what a particular sight or object prompts you to reflect.

There are probably two things people do that move the world. They are opposites and like the magnetic poles of the earth, they maintain the world in a balance that has far-reaching effects. Laughter and tears are those two things. Though we may not be flooding the oceans with our tears, there certainly isn't much laughter echoing in the sky. It is nice to think that *Pelón Drops Out* may bring laughter to someone's day. What can be healthier than organic insanity?

The book is fantasy. It may be an equally fantastic idea that this book is good enough to encourage people who do not read Spanish to make an attempt at understanding the few parts that are in Spanish. The author was born in California, learning both English and Spanish, as well as acquiring a third language which can best be described as off-the-wall. Why? Because it is a mixture of hip-trip English, street-Spanish and English words that are given a Spanish pronunciation. Chicanos have words that even a Spanish-speaking person would not understand unless he were bilingual.

The apprentices in the group formed a group to record a soundtrack for the book. Taking the book and the album to a promoter resulted in another failure to sell it, but the man was kind enough to offer his name for a jacket cover. We know the words from Frank Zippah will do much to endear this work to the teeny-boppers. Profesór Al Revés was nice enough to proof-read and correct Mr. Zippah's statement so it would be included without embarrassing his teachers.

Pelón Palomares

ABOUT THE ALBUM

by

Frank Zippah

and

the Flies

I was sitting in my giant quadrophonic office one day, relaxing to the tintillating Etta James and Sugar Pie de Santo, after a severe case of gastric distress at my having to eat The Carpenter's latest album which immobilized my pancreas. Oréja de Sordo, my music manager, was there auditioning Tony Baloney y Los Chorrizones, a new group from Texas in town for a performance at Brazo de Lápiz Tortilleria. They were accompanied by their velvet-voiced singer, the former señorita Llamada Carachorriada.

My secretary and main masseuse, Henrietta Handjive, was taking dictation from my lawyer, Charlie Chueco, regarding a new venture into the business world by my company, Mañaco Manufacturers. A friend of mine, Alveto Corcha, designed a new electric conga drum which can be used as a hanging plant-holder when not plugged in. I was interested in it as a possible new product for Mañaco Manufacturers.

All of a sudden, the walls ceased to vibrate with the thrilling reverberations of Etta's bassman. The speakers which serve as walls for my office crackled and popped like a giant box of Rice Krispies as the last electrical charges filtered out through the crevices in the burlap-covered grillework protecting the speakers from damage by Carey Karate and his partner, King-Kong Fúchi. They rent my office after hours, practicing their martial-arts mayhem until one a.m. when the cleaning lady comes in to grab them by the ring around their collars, ejecting them as she has been doing for the past two months.

I must admit I was the most surprised of all when the door was shattered by the force of Pelón's stride as he came bopping into my office to present me with a microfilmed copy of his latest book. He carried the microscopic *opus magnum* beneath a band-aid, fearing a mugger might rob him of his precious possession. Having known Pelón for some time and recognizing his intense need for immediate action, I hastily commanded everyone to leave the office. I broke my brand new Captain Cucaracha ring as my fist crashed down atop the desk to accentuate my order.

Frantically turning the pages of the specially treated paper which expanded to normal size upon contact with the atmosphere, I read the manuscript as fast as my lips could move; lest Pelón become angry and grab me by my trademark. I looked up with glazed eyes, shaken to the very max of my maxed-out mind, only to discover that Pelón had left the office with everyone else. He always likes to do as he is told, winning him the annual Kindergarten teacher's award for Admirable Adjustment four years in a row.

Peeking out through the splintered remains of my doorway, my astounded eyes fell upon the muscular maniac, peeping, "What can I do for you today my friend?" The demented cement mason's fierce countenance appeared inches from my terror-stricken orbs, destroying my six-day deodorant pads with the ultra-violent rays emitted by his intimidating eyes.

Pelón stormed into my office, grabbed the manuscript off the desk and waved it in his left hand like a Bowie knife. His right hand formed an imaginary pistol as he pointed to my chair, growling, "Sit down there and listen, you slimy leftover from a Black Widow spider's wedding reception. I got some business to talk over with you, even though you don't know chips from Shinola about making money. Look at you! Don't you ever get any sun or exercise? What do you do, lift drumsticks and play Colonel Sander's bucket? I've seen electric cords with more muscles than you display when you're on stage, giving the little Suzie's their not-so-cheap thrills." He roared as I sat trembling, wondering how many more decibels the windows could take.

"Okay," Pelón uttered, his voice dropping in volume as he sat on the desk, spinning me in my chair to face him by gently jerking on my goatee. "See this bunch of papers? If it ain't a bone-fried and guaranteed bestseller within a couple of years when the bozos catch on, I'll eat your apostrophe! You can buy it, *cheap.* Stick one of your crummy records inside the book cover. Pass it out to the high-schoolers with a free treasure map leading to the location of the hidden dope. Lace the grooves of the electronic screeching you call music with some kind of chemical that addicts them to your maniacal music and tell them, *lick it, it's yummy and will make you forget mummy.*"

"This book is so sharp you can cut umbilical cords with it. You can become the latest Pied Piper of America's youth. But if I catch you poisoning those kids with any hot nasties, I'll pull your curlies out, one at a time. I'll make a wigged-out dummy with your face on it so the police recruits can practice their billyclub technique."

"You can take it to the Brown Buffalo and say, *eat your heart out Chump-with-a-Hump.* Tell him you found this book soaking up the oil underneath Milo Menso's '54 Chevy. Tell him the only reason it has dirty words in it is because the author couldn't afford one of those Andy Granatelli Double Double Filters for his typewriter. Put a little coin in my pocket as a down-payment and I'll modify, codify, wrangle and mangle this work of art into a neat piece of junk you can sell at a nice profit."

"What do you think Sport?" inquired Pelón, ending his tirade. He patted me tenderly on the back as he wiped the overspray from my shirt, which was moist from having suffered through his adenoidal attack.

Well, it was tempting, I must admit. But this guy is loonier than I am. I don't need any competition. I have enough trouble, finding it harder and harder to find anything revolting enough to outshine all the new stars threatening my status. At least the dude could have said he liked my new album, *Cruising in my '55 Buick Roadmonster with Lencho and Lola* (available at your local music store on the Guru-Vee label).

I put on my best all-American businessman's act and said with as much sincerity as possible, "It sounds fascinating, *really*, it does. It's far-in and psycho-delirious, *heavy,* a mind-blower, blah, blah, etc., etc. But I have a lot of work to do. My mom wants me home for dinner no later than five, I have to see my dentist for a refill at 11:30, a luncheon engagement with my accountant at 1:30, band rehearsal at 7:30. Gee Pelón, you can see I don't have much time to read your book all the way through just now. Can you come back on . . . . . . let's see. . . . . . I have an opening in my appointment book for the twenty-third of August, can you come back then?"

Well kids, I won't repeat what that Communist said. But I want to ask you a favor. And ask your mummy and daddy too. Please don't read his book. Take my word for it, it's crummy tasting like Listerine and nasty like my mouth on Sunday morning after a Hollywood party. Besides, that guy's so crazy, he might start his own band or hire Tower of Power to back him. Then where would I be? I have a lot of payments to make you know!

I'll always look mangy for you. I'll continue producing screechie music so you can turn the volume up real loud and drive mummy and daddy to the liquor store.

> Bye bye and a bunch of RPM's,
> Your loyal and trusty friend
>
> Frank "Witch-I-Were" Zippah
> Executive Vice-President
> Lotsa Noise, unlimited
> (A subsidiary of Pestoso Platters, Inc.)

PELON DROPS OUT

PELON DROPS OUT

CHAPTER UNO

"Do not divulge to anyone the secrets I will share with you during your apprenticeship, Pelón," cautioned Gerónimo Vidrios, master mason, his voice a murmur barely audible above the shrill imitations of a Mockingbird whistling at the early morning sun.

Pelón strained to hear the shirt-sleeved warrior, his own body shivering beneath layers of clothing his mother had commanded he wear before leaving the house to greet the morning sun's first irridescent rays. The sack Pelón held in his tiny fist spoke to him of its warm contents; the tacos and pan dulce his mother insisted he take that first day of work. At least with the rolled tortillas filled with beans and meat and the sweet bread, Pelón was partially prepared for his initiation into the secretive and tradition-bearing world known intimately by the older masters.

His mother's concerned voice echoed through his mind as Pelón struggled to keep pace with the seemingly tireless Gerónimo whose shoulders appeared as massive obstacles preventing the sun's smile from caressing the cold earth. The bull-necked maestro walked effortlessly across the expanse of pathless dirt, stepping over holes and mounds with the demeanor of a deer. Pelón's new workshoes felt like a deep-sea diver's equipment as he stumbled clumsily over large dirt clods, his mother's sweet voice in his mind.

"Watch out for the cu-cui and don't talk to the pachucos on your way home from work," he heard. His mother's warning came from a rock-lined chamber in his mind as he studied the movement of Gerónimo with confused intensity. He unsuccessfully copied Gerónimo's stride, nearly falling over a pile of dirt left by some scheming laborer to trip the aspiring apprentice.

They were walking across the area of unfinished apartments, the buildings circling the future recreation center were in various stages of construction. Some were plastered, others waited for the plasterers, wearing a black-paper and wire-mesh shirt to protect their wooden frames from the weather. A tractor was parked nearby, a shallow indentation in the ground outlining the spot where it would soon be digging the dirt out for a swimming pool. Pelón was lost in this new world of construction he had entered in hopes of discovering new frontiers of knowledge at the feet of the locally renowned masters of concrete work.

He had begun his apprenticeship, pledging his utmost to learn the business of laying concrete sidewalks, pool decks, steps and other types of concrete work found around buildings. Pelón had heard rumors that the work of the maestros was but a front, a subterfuge for their real sideline as brujos. Pelón had sought out Gerónimo, wanting to join the maestro in learning the trade, but more importantly, to learn the other secrets that Gerónimo and a few others were said in whispers to possess.

"Do not step on the ditch!" sternly warned Gerónimo, his fierce eyes striking with paralyzing force on the nervous newcomer.

"Somebody spent a lot of time digging. They don't want you covering up their work before they've had a chance to install the plastic sprinkler lines, cabeza de calabasa," stated Gerónimo, calling Pelón a pumpkin-head. "Come on snowshoes, quit walking around like you still have your pajamas and slippers on," hissed the maestro. His gait made short work of the distance to his truck. The flatbed truck was parked near a brick wall, tools and lumber on the back of the vehicle visible to the bewildered apprentice.

"You're liable to mess up somebody's work and they'll put the curse of the mal ojo on you," gravely cautioned Gerónimo. Pelón shuddered at the thought of someone casting an evil eye on him as he tripped over a stack of stakes. The wooden lengths of sharpened wood ascended from their hiding place on the ground to grab menacingly at his feet.

"Unload that wheelbarrow and shovel. Follow me," growled the impatient maestro, walking away from the confused neophyte. Gerónimo did not seem to care if his commands were understood or not.

"Well, come on knucklehead, are you gonna take all day, or what?" Pelón heard as the weighty wheelbarrow pushed him viciously, its spirit angered at being touched by an inexperienced fool.

Watching in wonder, Gerónimo screamed at the uncoordinated Pelón who weeks earlier had asked him for a job as a helper.

"Hey, Professor Backwards, get your carcass in gear and get over here so I can show you what I want graded out," roared Gerónimo at the puzzled Pelón. The apprentice was trying not to groan as the wheelbarrow uncooperatively cracked against his shin-bone. He fought the bucking and resolute monster who refused to be pushed around by the ignorant rookie. The angry wheelbarrow vowed to have its brother, the shovel, punish Pelón for having had the effrontery to wedge its wheel into a ditch.

"Hijo del maíz," sighed Gerónimo to the clouds. His words were a ceremonial plea to the mist, asking for strength that he might endure the challenge the day promised. He would need much patience with Pelón who had so much to learn.

"Where's the pick? Don't tell me you expect to dig out an entryway between apartments without a pick," groaned the maestro, unable to fathom the apprentice's ignorance.

"Never mind, get back here," called Gerónimo. The retreating Pelón stopped. The fleeing Indian froze in his tracks, the dazed dumbbell stopping before he could hurdle a mound of sand left by the plasterers.

"Pay attention now," commanded Gerónimo, glancing to his left to smile a barely detectable greeting to his friend and fellow maestro, Santos Trigeño.

The cheerful Santos materialized from out of nowhere before the befuddled Pelón who scrutinized the area for a place Santos may have been hiding to make his timely entrance. Grasping the shovel in salute to the spirit of sweat, the amiable Santos asked Gerónimo's permission to show the recruit his first secret of the trade.

"Watch carefully, piernas de ormiga," smiled the comical character as he assumed one of the positions taught him by another maestro. Some day he would tell the ant-legged Pelón of that time long ago when the magical air and laughing plants had spoken to him of their secrets. It was some years since they had pleased Santos with their tickly touches on his rippling stomach. His center of power was then but a dry cell battery compared to the multimillion watt storage plant he now possessed.

"This is your first friend. You must speak to it kindly. Tell it of your wish to know its secrets. Perhaps it will take a liking to you. I'm sure it will, I can see how your legs resemble it. I am confident that if you ask properly, its spirit will merge with your own. Piernas de ormiga are a good omen," spoke Santos happily as he turned to his friend Gerónimo. His blink was a perfect imitation of an owl.

"Use the pointed edge of the square shovel to break the hard dirt," instructed Santos, his surprisingly strong thrusts quickly taking their toll. The hard-packed dirt soon yielded, falling like scattered pieces of bread from a broken loaf.

Gerónimo stood with his hands on his hips, admiring his friend's skill. His face assumed a frightening stare when Pelón's eyes left the object of his first lesson to glance at Gerónimo.

"Don't look at me with those fluttering pestañas!" The maestro glared at Pelón, whose eyelashes had indeed been fluttering as he gazed at the formidable Gerónimo.

"Pay attention, bird-body! You have to look until you learn what it is you are seeing," spoke the maestro harshly. "Santos does not show just anybody how to use the shovel properly. You better quit messing around and pay attention or you'll work yourself to death. You'll be sorry if you don't take this lesson seriously, cabeza de cacahuate," he warned the peanut-headed Pelón.

Gerónimo addressed the apprentice in the manner handed down through generations. The maestro was faithfully following the ways of his ancestors who were expert nicknamers. One had to be astute and observant, studying a person carefully to find just the right nickname. It may have been part of their Indian heritage, prompting them to usually create nicknames having something to do with animals. Occasionally, a person was given an organic or even mineral name.

"Has he learned the dance of the chicas patas?" inquired Santos. The maestro mirthfully began a harmonious chant as his feet stomped the chunks of earth. It was said that the chicas patas, little feet, were descendants of giants who long ago roamed the earth, forming the mountains and the valleys with their footsteps. The chicas patas, oral history said, came into being when the Creator decided to shrink the huge nomads. They were using too many animal skins for their huaraches and causing an imbalance in the ecology so God sent a special shrinking rain. It rained for many months and the giants grew smaller and smaller, no longer able to crush mountains beneath their feet.

Santos' talented talones rhythmically pounded the dirt clods into submission. Santos' agility surprised the young Pelón who stood aside in dumb appreciation of the maestro's movements. He was especially adept with his heels, twisting his feet as he stomped so his talones would both crush and compact the dirt.

"Pelón is too weak, his body too flabby," noted Gerónimo. "The dance of the chicas patas will have to come later. We must wait for his body to break the chains of imprisonment his mind's laziness has imposed on him. Perhaps later in the day we can let him eat the chilepuro so that he can feel its spirit move him from his mind's confinement."

"We must not try to teach him too much at one time," continued Gerónimo. "He is still under the spell of the cesos de caca," added the maestro.

The master noted that Pelón needed the help of a powerful ally to break the constipating effects of having been hexed by brainy academicians. Pelón would be a good pupil, thought Gerónimo. He knew instinctively that a true warrior clothed himself in a veil of mystery. The master had been forced to consult a bruta whose powers surpassed those of his own, begging his wife to consult the sacred chisme regarding the apprentice's past.

Gerónimo's wife, Ana Marana, had counseled with the elite group of women who daily gathered to drink steaming cups of yerba buena and canela. They drank tea from the honored herbs, letting the leaves give them information within the territory with amazing alacrity.

It was Gerónimo's wife who had divulged Pelón's past. She told him of the hypnotic stage Pelón would have to be carefully extricated from in order to begin whittling away at the lesser spells which remained to separate the young man from their reality.

Gerónimo was glad the young Chicano had come to him, seeking his help in becoming a warrior. He would not have liked to see Pelón going to the quacks and pretenders who thoughtlessly sold their secrets to the hippies. The hippies had even come to bother Gerónimo, the powerful and dreaded maestro himself.

Gerónimo studied the apprentice with a practiced eye. Pelón's body hinted of slumbering strength and emasculated endurance which would have to be freed of the weight of meaningless and silly thoughts. A warrior could not afford to pursue any but the path with meaning. Being a Chicano, Pelón had a good chance of becoming such a pathfinder. His blood was a mixture of European and Indian.

"Here," smiled Santos, handing Pelón the shovel after a few minutes of exuberant dance. His spirit had climbed lofty peaks of unsurpassed grandeur, climbing higher, ever higher. His heart was almost unable to stand the pace of his journey into the fifth world where reality was beyond dimension, above time, wider than an infinity of heavens.

Gerónimo's quiet call to Santos only faintly reminded the friendly maestro of his still to be severed ties with the first reality, but the call was heeded, bringing Santos back from his travels. He returned from his voyage on a sea of majestically crashing waves, through layers of conscious fantasy which caressingly soothed his warrior's spirit as he decompressed before returning to the world of work.

"There's nothing to it," chuckled Santos as Pelón's foot

missed the mark. The friendly shovel had assumed the spirit of
an opponent and dodged Pelón's mighty kick. His foot was
pulled from its target by invisible tentacles wrapping themselves
around his sinewy ankle. The sharp steel grazed along his instep
in flagrant disregard of his feelings.

"A warrior does not show pain!" bellowed Gerónimo. The
maestro's voice resounded through the cave-like entryway like a
lion's roar. Pelón forgot the pain as he jumped from the sudden
jolt of the menacing maestro's yell.

Santos rolled on the ground, shaking spasmodically on his
back. His legs kicked frantically as he tried to contain the laughter that was bursting at his center of power. He held his hands
over his navel, holding in the vibrant fibers straining at his om-
bligo, lest they reach out with uncontrollable force in response
to his mirth. He could not risk harming the young apprentice
who as yet lacked the power to contend with the dangerous om-
bligo lines.

Pelón labored through the morning, determined to copy the
master's example. He addressed the earth with respect, vocally
when no strangers were about, and silently when a plumber or
electrician would approach. He could no longer claim to be an
inhabitant of the ordinary world of these men.

By midday, the wheelbarrow had reluctantly agreed to ease
its battle against Pelón. A truce of sorts was reached as Pelón
again and again brought it gifts of dirt to appease its appetite.
The shovel's spirit was beginning to change its behavior. The
traces of its new role as his friend were beginning to manifest
themselves. The tributary perspiration Pelón presented in sub-
servience throughout the long morning's initiation was grate-
fully acknowledged by the shovel and accepted by the earth.
The shovel promised Pelón he would have no permanent scars
from their first encounter. They would be friends.

"You have done well, my son," murmured Santos. The
hopeful recruit rested by a mound of bricks, munching a burri-
to. Pelón's heart swelled as Santos' compliment injected inspira-
tion into his tired body. He was a dirigible being filled with gas,
expanding to the limits of its steel skin.

"You must not expect Gerónimo to treat you in any other way than that of a stern teacher. It is his modo, his nature, to be gruff. It is because he cares not about caring. He does not let things matter, though they are of importance. It is the warrior's way. Caring, yet unable to let things matter, the task at hand being the only thing of true consequence for the moment."

Santos spoke softly, a suggestion of heartfelt memories and timeless recollections clouding his eyes as he spoke, his words floating to Pelón's ears like the delicate flight of a butterfly. The tender words coaxing their way through his ears imperceptibly changed as Pelón looked at Santos. The misty-eyed maestro issued a loud burp and the delicate butterfly buzzed like a bee in his ears.

Santos continued addressing the discouraged apprentice who had allowed Gerónimo's screams and pretended threats to puncture his untempered armor. Placing a fatherly hand on the sad young warrior's shoulder, Santos spoke in a whisper. Gerónimo stood nearby, his ears perking up like a deer catching the scent of a grizzly in the autumn air as he tuned in on the conversation.

"You have shown great fortitude and resolution in this morning's quest for knowledge. Come, I will let you taste the first mixture which you will have to take and learn about in your future bouts with your spirit's opponents."

Santos whispered secretively, motioning with his left eyelid for Pelón to follow. Pelón was more than mildly surprised at the vocabulary these men possessed. He was pleased that he had ventured to risk the unknown in approaching the feared but respected Gerónimo. He was glad that Gerónimo's partner, Santos, had taken a liking to him.

"The world's first level of reality forces me to use this plastic thermos, but I feel confident the spirit of the mixture has not been altered by its containment by unnatural forces," said Santos seriously. He squatted gracefully before the interested Pelón who examined the wide-mouthed thermos. The spirit of the wind gently coaxed the aroma of the mixture into his flared nostrils.

"Wait," cautioned Santos, his hand rising quickly to halt Pelón in mid-progress as he tilted the thermos to his lips. Santos looked at Gerónimo who had quietly approached, standing next to them with an inscrutable face. His muscular arms crossed his expansive chest.

"Con permiso," murmured Santos, his eyes closing. In a traditional manner, he asked permission of Gerónimo to instruct the apprentice in another aspect of their knowledge. Gerónimo shrugged.

"I must first speak a few words over the mixture, my son. You are too impatient. Gerónimo may be right. You may not be a suitable student," he stated, crushing Pelón beneath an avalanche of sadness as Santos' words formed ice on the wings of his eager spirit.

"I am sorry maestro. I shall not do it again. I promise," vowed Pelón. He desperately searched for words which might adequately convey his sincere wish to be a satisfactory apprentice.

"A man does not make promises!" thundered Gerónimo. The master turned his back on Pelón. The grief-stricken candidate stood dumbly, unable to comprehend the events unfolding before him. The earth trembled beneath his weakened body as his disappointment sapped his strength.

"It is of no consequence," comforted Santos. His hand was extended palm upward in a signal of humble acceptance of the ways of youth. "You will learn the manner of a warrior. It will be difficult; a hard road for someone so impatient as you. The boulders do not move aside with the mere wave of the hand. It takes much power, much will to accomplish such feats my son. It takes . . . . . ."

"Puro pedo!" came Gerónimo's cloud-moving voice.

"Exactly. Gracias, Gerónimo, I could not remember the Spanish words for this phenomenon," explained Santos who had hesitated. The master had stopped to think if it were wise to give Pelón the English equivalents that described this most important aspect of a warrior's power.

"I myself have known many sorrows in my travels toward the ultimate destiny," continued Santos. His eyes again suggested a myriad of deeply felt emotions to the impressed Pelón.

"I even had to *fight* my way at times. No, the ways of a warrior are harder than your young and innocent mind can imagine. You are here because you heard a call, a beckoning sound that pulled your spirit until now you are here with us. Listen, perhaps you will hear that sound again," he whispered, his finger pointing to the sky.

"What did you hear?" came Santos' coaxing voice. His inquiry had the patience of a thousand years of peering through hypnotic haze in search for the unseeable land of the unknown.

Pelón was afraid to speak, stuttering frightfully as he fought to say what his mind commanded his voice to utter. He fought within himself against overwhelming odds, forcing out the words which were sure to bring the ire of the maestros upon his fearful being. He had to say it, unable to deny what his ears and eyes, his nose, confirmed. Meekly, haltingly, he answered Santos.

"It was a fart."

"It was not a fart!" Gerónimo's voice shook the ground with even more violence than Santos' machinegun burst of air.

Santos was creating huge clouds of dust as he rolled spasmodically on the dirt, great squeals of laughter piercing the air. Men turned in their direction from different locales on the job. With superhuman effort, Santos resumed his squat position.

"You have very good ears and a reliable nose. You are not easily fooled," grunted Santos. "It is good. The way of a warrior demands that a true man of power have command of his senses," he stated decisively, holding the thermos with both hands as a priest holds a chalice.

"Do not ever repeat my words before a gavacho or anyone else not belonging to the world of working warriors," he sternly warned Pelón. The apprentice was surprised at Santos' sudden change in character.

"Listen. Your life may someday depend on it. Do not let

The chilepuro was indeed formidable.

these words be forgotten. Pass them on from one to another, as we are doing now. You will learn much more about the ways of true power and will. But for the moment, concentrate on my words. Let your spirit merge with the spirit of the wind, that it might carry you over continents. Let the wind take you so your spirit might merge with the spirit of the elephant. Let his ears be yours, that you might hear precisely. Let your eyes merge with those of the sharp-eyed eagle, that you might *see* what I am about to do. Prepare yourself well my son, it is a serious matter."

Holding the thermos as though it contained precious gems, Santos began to recite a litany in the gutteral voice of his Indian ancestors. The melody was a raspy harmony which Pelón avidly listened to. The maestro's voice blended with the lullaby of the breeze, hypnotizing the intent Pelón as he stared at the swaying Santos. The master's invocation had a strange effect on the curious recruit who did not know whether to remain standing or assume the pose of the squatting man who chanted before Pelón.

>Pelón, Pelón, Cabeza de Melón,
>piernas de mosca, muchacho cabezón.
>Brazos de ormiga, cesos de queso,
>naríz de zanahoria con mente de hueso.
>En esta junta hay una pregunta,
>cuando verás la verdad?
>Pa que sepas que estas tapado,
>le ofrezco lo embotellado,
>tomátelo con sinceridad.

>Pelón, Pelón, you melon head,
>you requested brains and received squash instead.
>Arms of a fly, head of a hatholder,
>a carrot nose with the brain of a boulder.

At this time there is one puzzle,
will you find the truth by taking a guzzle?
Your carburetor brain has a broken throttle,
I can fix it with the stuff in this bottle.
If you drink STP it will make you delirious,
but chilipuro is worse if you don't take it serious.

The master moaned in ritualistic communion with the spirit of spirits. Handing the thermos to Pelón with practiced movements, he whispered with closed eyes.

"Drink it quickly. Do not stop until it is all gone."

The spirit of the chilepuro slashed its way down his throat, meeting his terrified heart halfway on its trip towards Pelón's adam's apple. His fearful heart was making a last desperate attempt to escape the unknown.

The chilepuro was indeed formidable. Pelón would have to wait for another day to speak of its wonders. His voice was incapable of verbalizing, words denied his mouth for the rest of the afternoon as his body came close to exploding with newly found energy and strength. His mind broke through the first-layer-reality to take him headlong on his first battle with himself.

Even the stern Gerónimo could not contain his laughter as the chilepuro engulfed Pelón's digestive tract in flames calculated to release him from his chains. The chilepuro was designed to free his spirit which had been laboring under the shadow of the curse of the tapado. It was a special mixture intended to extricate him from his zombified state by uncoiling his intestines, the tripas and pipas that had to be unwound so as to chase away the cursed spell.

Pelón's eyes stung as a fierce battle waged between his weak body and the invincible power of the chilepuro. Cataclysmic sensations announced his legs' urge to run like a yearling. His untrained eyes searched everywhere, desperately darting about the construction site for a place of safety where he might privately deal with his war.

Laughter echoed eerily from the spot he had been standing on before his body left him to inhabit the cliffs of the eagle. From somewhere in the spinning galaxy of multicolored forms came a voice half-heartedly commanding through choking guffaws that he seek a remedy for the inferno melting the remnants of the tapado's curse.

"Drink some milk before you suffer an attack of chorro."

It was the voice of Santos, instructing Pelón to counteract the chilepuro's dauntless destruction with milk, to avoid having to exit the extraordinary world the apprentice had unknowingly entered; an antidote to postpone the warrior's departure with what can only be poorly translated into English as the *back-door-runs.*

Pelón, Pelón, Cabeza de Melón

PELON DROPS OUT

CHAPTER DOS

PELON DROPS OUT

Purple shadows outlined the mountains. An orange velvet
glow dawned as Pelón opened the back door of his house to
look. He walked into the chill of the new morning, his eyes
drawn to the nopal at the rear of the yard. The cactus had
many diamonds on its ears, glittering faintly in the soft light
of the creeping sunrise.

It would be a wonderful day, the sun turning yellow-gold
as it sent advance notice of its arrival over the distant peaks.
The moon was still visible on the horizon, stars were flashing
their last light on a silken film of changing colors. The air was
crisp and clear, rushing through his nose to speak to him of
the day's smells.

He retrieved his tool bucket from beneath a small patio
table where it had spent the night, the steel trowels protected
from the dampness. Pelón took the bucket of tools to his car.
Walking back to the kitchen, he left his car's engine idling, a
white cloud of exhaust escaping the confinement of the metal
pipe to disappear in the cold morning air.

His mother's hands tossed and turned in a slapping synthesis, converting the masa into round tortillas which she placed
gingerly on the hot griddle to be gently toasted. Pelón
reached for the paper sack containing his freshly made lunch.
His mother put the tupperware container of masa in the refrigerator, saving the dough for later when she would make
more tortillas.

Mrs. Palomares was still upset that Pelón had refused to
take his new lunch-pail to work. It was such a nice lunch-pail,
why did he insist on taking the tacos out of the nice lunch-
pail and put them in a sack? She had chosen it herself, thinking her son would like to carry his lunch in the brightly
painted box depicting John Wayne in a shoot-out with cattle
rustlers. It even showed the hero sitting down to a hearty
meal at the chuckwagon.

Pelón turned through the kitchen door before remembering to drink his glass of orange juice and raw eggs. He placed
the empty glass back on the kitchen counter, his hand reach-

ing again for the doorknob. It was but a small sacrifice for
him to forego a real breakfast. Pelón's mother worked very
hard taking care of the family. The juice and eggs would see
him through the morning.

"Que Dios te bendiga mi'jo. Don't talk to the pachucos
and watch out for the cu-cui," she called patiently as he de-
parted. She crossed herself in silent request that God protect
her son. Pelón visualized the pachucos whom his mother daily
warned him against, and he was unable to create an image of
what the terrible cu-cui might look like. He could not picture
the formless monster which threatened unwary people who
ventured into the night where it lurked. It seemed odd that
his mother should still fear her son's contact with the pachucos. Pelón drove a car now and did not have to walk the
streets of La Oya where the gang-members hung out.

"Hey, hey! Help me get these tools off the truck," yelled
Fly'nn Calabera, his angular body straining as he pulled a
heavy wheelbarrow from the flatbed truck. The lanky Fly'nn
Calabera reminded Pelón of an Afghanistan hound, his hirsute
leanness prompting Pelón to accuse the sad-eyed lad of wearing a permanent mohair sweater.

"Why don't you just back the truck real fast and pound
your leadfoot on the brake, cuerpo de lasso. Save a lot of
trouble that way," grunted Pelón as he reached for some
tools. His stomach pressed into the metal-reinforced bed of
the truck as he leaned over to grasp the tamp. He was happy
to have acquired the maestro's manner of expression, remembering how dull his language was before meeting the color-
fully speaking cement masons.

"Last time he tried that, he forgot to hit the brake and almost ended up tunneling through a building like a super-
termite digging through balsa wood," observed Tiburón. Gerónimo's son bounded by the truck, using a shovel like a pogo
stick. Tiburón's tusks gleamed in the sunlight, reminding
Pelón that the nickname of Shark was in honor of his famous
smile.

"Here comes Super-Spiffy to the rescue!" screamed Bambi, announcing his incoming flight to the astounded group of
apprentices. The momentum of his body as he ran full speed
toward the truck sent him through the air when his feet
tripped over the curb. It was a magnificent flight, launched
with breath-taking velocity as he left the runway. His trajectory was intercepted by the truck's lumber-rack, where he was
at present spinning wildly. Bambi gripped the rack in a fear-
some hold until finally revolving to a stop.

"Hijo, what the heck you call that trick, cuerpo de
clavo," queried Spanicy as he and Cockroach ambled in their
direction. "I thought you were pretending to be a dive-bomb-
ing crow when I saw you hit that curb and take off like a
pencil shot out of a cannon," added Spanicy in disbelief at
the gravity-defying leap he had witnessed.

"I didn't really trip. It was my plan from the very beginning," explained Bambi.

The thin apprentice's eyelids were fluttering rapidly as he
realized the magnitude of his feat. Tiburón gazed with wonder
at the magnitude of Bambi's feet.

"Did you take a picture with your polarized peppers,
Pelón? Let me look in your ear while you concentrate and
put your brain on rewind," instructed Bambi as he extended a
long arm. His claw-like hand tenaciously grasped Pelón's ear.
He pulled the hesitant Pelón toward him.

"Wow, look at that! I just saw an X-rated movie!" he exclaimed as he dug a slender finger into Pelón's ear to clear the
projector of some wax coating on the lens.

"Get away, leave me alone!" hollered Pelón as the anxious
apprentices fought for their turn at the arcade. Tapping his
foot as he bent his right pectoral, Pelón assumed the position
of unassailable power which Santos only recently had taught
him. The group recoiled rapidly, knowing the potential power
of their fellow recruit.

"If you guys don't stop messing around, I'm gonna give
you the old triple cauamalámcondingdong," he threatened.

His left hand remolded his ear to a facsimile of its former shape.

"Don't let the maestros hear you say that," intoned Ricky Rock. He sauntered up to the group, chewing some nails in order to fashion a ring for his girlfriend. "That's serious business and you shouldn't be fooling around with your ding-dong," he mumbled through crunching jaws.

The ground began shaking, ominously shifting to warn the soon-to-be warriors that something was amiss. The stirring of the earth was violent, stopping their prankish behavior. They looked at each other in wide-eyed wonder. New fissures were split into the earth's entrails, old cracks and wrinkles nearly torn asunder. They collectively uttered the words which they knew would explain the quaking of the earth.

"It's the boss," they exhaled in one voice. Their knees clattered in a skeleton dance as they looked in every direction for the fearful figure's approach.

"I wanna go home," whimpered Bambi from his hiding place beneath a pile of lumber.

"I already left," came Spanicy's muffled remark from his shelter beneath an overturned wheelbarrow. The steel shell's size nine shape was not quite adequate to conceal Spanicy's size twenty body. Only his closed eyes kept the illusion of concealment. He moaned through chattering teeth, looking like a frightened turtle whose shell was shrunk by the cleaners.

"Don't sweat it. Where else can you become a man of power and a fearless warrior while you earn money?" spoke Tiburón with little conviction in his trembling voice. As the son of the main maestro, he felt obliged to bolster the courage of the intimidated rookies. Tiburón gave his pep talk from under the hood of the truck where he had dived desperately. He wasn't actually scared. He was only checking the motor mounts.

"You mocosos get over here! Right now!" roared a rock-splitting voice. The startled group jumped from their hiding places in heart-stopping surprise, bumping into one another. They tumbled over each other as they frantically searched for the spot from which the volcano had beckoned their sniveling presence.

"Line up according to height and in alphabetical order before I get mad and put a brain in those pointed heads!" came the loudspeaker voice of Gerónimo as he miraculously appeared before the befuddled bozos. His towering form emerged from behind a cloud of dust created by their mad scrambling.

Pelón, Ricky Rock, Bambi, Tiburón, Jr., Cockroach and Fly'nn Calabera stood at attention before the glaring master. Spanicy was struggling to peel the too-tight wheelbarrow from his back. The metal protuberance adhering to his rear was equal in prominence to the mass hanging over his belt buckle. Finally, with a popping sound, Spanicy was free to join the apprentices.

"Do not let confusion reign supreme or let the rain confuse you with its idle chatter," comforted Santos. The friendly maestro appeared from behind the terrifying master as Gerónimo posed against the sun like Attila the Hun outside the gates of Rome.

"You have all been preparing yourselves for some time now, learning the ways of the world that will make you warriors whose armor cannot be pierced by the petty concerns of ordinary reality," spoke Santos. His sharp eyes glanced from one nervous youth to another, surveying the young initiates who stood before him. Santos carefully scrutinized his fellow travelers on the path to knowing.

Pelón listened to the soft-spoken master, studying the powerfully built dark-haired man. His words reminded Pelón of the tedious hours of training and practice the apprentices had undergone in the three months since Pelón had first been introduced to their world. It was a fantastically fabricated world of perception which the two men described to him during each day's lesson.

Tightening his stomach muscles in an effort to summon his will, Pelón fought off the traces of fear threatening to slow his progress toward the goal. Pelón recalled how he foolishly interpreted the stirring in his abdominal region as hunger, before the two instructors had taught him differently.

The leaves waving on the windblown branches of the nearby sycamores were no longer vegetable matter whose colors changed as they flapped in the sun's brightness. They were a curtain of glowing beads through which his spirit would enter a magnificent world where nopales talked. Cacti would smile their invitation to Pelón, urging him to join their play in the centuries old games.

His body was responding. The acrid chilepuro no longer became a raging prairie fire leaving his internal organs to blister and smolder in the aftermath of a horrendous fire-storm. His eyes would no longer blind him with stinging tears as he ingested the chilepuro. They would allow him to see as his spirit exited its human form to merge with the vibrating and shimmering curtain separating him from the first chamber lying beyond his ordinary state of reality. Santos looked at Pelón who had temporarily let his attention wander from the first reality.

Pelón let his mind create a vision transmitting a scene to his being in which another Pelón, accompanied by his new friends, parted the silvery-shadowed curtain to embark on another journey into unimaginable landscapes of sparkling crystaline forms. He was going into the land of conscious Chicanismo, the place of being and non-bean.

"You must not wander too far from the present," murmured the mellow voice of Santos.

He gently addressed the daydreaming student, his face appearing inches from Pelón's rapturously detached countenance. Santos quietly halted Pelón's precipitous entry into other worlds of universal dissimilarity.

"Pelón, you are perhaps the most capable of the group of aspiring apprentices here today. Your mind is quick to grasp

the intricacies and subtlties of our ways. Though you may not
be gifted so awesomely as the others, your body is adequate.
You will do well in the next test. Your wits and cleverness
will persevere. I know it in my heart," whispered the kind
maestro.

A faint smile was detectable in Santos' squinting eyes as
his sometimes comical face came between Pelón and the distant trees whose call the apprentice was on the verge of answering. They had not swallowed their day's portion of chilepuro nor smoked the mixture of verdolagas, ojas de elote and
tolondrones pa' los preguntones. Pelón had yet to smoke this
mixture. Today would be his first meeting with the carefully
blended friend.

But already the iron-willed maestro's eyes were having
their curious effect on the unbelieving Pelón who stood mute-
ly observing the phantasmagoric scene unveiling within Santos'
eyes. Santos' ojitos seemingly enveloped Pelón, carrying him
off on a thrilling adventure to forget where his body remained. His mind was unable to comprehend the strange
sensations the flight made his new body a witness to.

The ascent into another reality unnerved him to the point
where he could no longer know if he was moving rapidly or
frozen to the spot. Pelón felt a misty, vaporous stream of
spirit leaving his body. It merged with the figure he was
mysteriously observing in a trance-like moment of extraordinary realism.

Pelón was no longer a part of the world in which he daily
operated, leaving to join the Pelón of some other universe
through the doorway of Santos' incredible ojitos. The master's
mystical eyes stopped the earth's turning, luring the hesitant
warrior's spirit from its hibernation deep within the apprentice.

Pelón heard a name echoed by the mountains, their massive presence softened by the gold hue of their cloak in the
summer sun. The warrior turned in recognition of the new
name which struck with familiarity on his soul. His true name

resounded through the canyons, floating to greet the treetops as the wind embraced and scattered the particles of sound to the sky.

"Chopopóte."

It came to him with timeless clarity, unknown in its origin, yet striking a chord within his responsive heart. The name was a reminder of his eternal existence within age-old worlds which served as a backdrop for his ceaseless wanderings along the path of truth.

"Chopopóte," hissed the rattlesnake in salute.

"Chopopóte," howled the timberwolf to his friend.

The mighty warrior leaped from the desert floor to stand atop a pine-covered mountain, surveying the grandeur below. He saw the eagle before he heard it whistle his name. Its broad wings played with the wind as it soared above.

"Chopopóte," came the eagle's shrill cry. "Please join me. We will fly to the sun and offer homage to our grandfather. Spread your wings my friend. The magic of our brother the sky will clothe you in golden feathers that you might come with me on an exciting flight to where you have already been. You were there, many years ago, when your warrior's spirit was but an innocent child protected by us. Close your eyes and let the breeze release you from the caress of the mountains my brother. It is but a matter of wanting."

"Chopopóte," came the bird's soft plea. "Forget you care. Do not let yourself desire to want. A warrior desires nothing but to be. That is the secret. That is what ties you to your grandmother's apron strings, holding you to the earth."

"Chopopóte," called the stallion from the glowing desert floor. "My brother, I am glad to see you. There are no warriors brave enough to ride me. You are the last one. I miss the excitement of galloping to the crest of the mountains with a true warrior on my back to urge me on. Run, my brother, run. Let the wind's spirit give speed to your feet that you might catch me," came the friendly challenge from the magnificent stallion. His front hooves towered above the desert as he called to the warrior.

Chopopóte.

"Aiyee!" screamed the shirtless brave, his muscles gleaming in bronzed splendor.

"I shall see you another time, brother eagle. I must ride the wind and have a moment with my brother the horse," he called as he mightily flung himself from the mountain-top. Hurdling over boulders, dodging trees, he made his way down the shrubbed sides of the canyons. He could hear the stallion's delightful laugh as he pursued the elusive horse.

Bounding over manzanita, jumping with superhuman strides through the desert in pursuit of the speeding stallion—lightning trying to capture the thunder. Brother stallion disappeared around a bend. Chopopóte scrambled up the side of a canyon to reach the top, leaping in a dazzling arc from the hilltop to land atop the startled stallion's back.

The warrior's grip proved too much for the astounded horse. He could not break his friend's hold on his mane. The stallion bucked and twisted for what seemed forever to the delight of the creatures witnessing the friendly battle. In a few seconds, the stallion would make a run for it, seeing that Chopopóte was not as easy to throw as a puma. A fierce gallop would do the trick, thought the proud stallion as he arched his back. Throwing himself viciously into the air in a last attempt to shake Chopopóte, they took off on a breathtaking run.

"Pelón! Do not enter the other world until you are ready. Fool, you could be trapped, never to return," admonished Gerónimo.

"While you were away, I dismissed the others with their instructions for the day. They each know their task. Now we shall prepare you for another step along the path to power."

"Soon, a mechanical monster will arrive. The seriousness of this business makes it necessary for you to dispatch as quickly as possible this dangerous threat to our profits. This monster eats up time and we have taught you that in this trade, time is money," said Gerónimo, bringing Pelón back to reality.

"Your body has learned much. It is stronger now. You will pick up this mechanical monster and shake it with all your might. You must summon your will. Ask your friends for their assistance. You will need all the help you can get to empty the mechanical monster of its cargo. It carries in its iron belly the wet concrete that will serve to make you totally stoned."

Santos stepped comically towards the pair, returning from the truck where he had retreated when he saw that Pelón was embarked on an adventure. Santos decided it was time to return to the pupil's side as Gerónimo rousted the apprentice from his fantastic travel. Santos handed Pelón a strangely formed cigarette whose outer skin was like rough parchment.

"It is time for you to smoke the powerful mixture that will give you the strength of giants. You will need its assistance when the mechanical monster arrives, my son. You must smoke all of it. When you are through, we shall give you a little chile-puro. It will help ease the effects of the mixture in the cigarette, in case the mixture is not in a good mood."

"Attack! You must not give the monster any quarter. Pick it up and shake with all your might. Do not let your spirit be overpowered. If you lose this battle, how do you expect to do against the most formidable opponent of all, el cu-cui. Even I, a true warrior, have had to back down from the cu-cui on occasion. It is no laughing matter. That is why you must smoke the mixture. It will prepare you for the mechanical monster and any future encounters with the cu-cui."

Pelón examined the odd-shaped cigarette, remembering that Santos had earlier described its contents. Santos had explained they could not use a sacred pipe because there were strangers about; gavachos who would not understand the ritual pipe-passing. They were people who would not know the ways of a warrior and would seek to destroy their movidas, their rites.

Santos had gone on to tell Pelón of the many hippies seeking to buy the mixture from the knowledgeable maestros. The begging, the urging of the hippies who wanted to possess the sacred verdolagas and tolondrones pa' los preguntones; wanting to know the secrets of the oja de elote. They did not know the importance and significance of the ingredients. They were fools playing with destiny, wanting to become warriors and men of power without working at it in the traditional manner.

Slapping at Pelón's outstretched hand, Santos began his ritualistic chant, ignoring the impatient youth. He throatily exhorted the spirit of the mixture to manifest itself as Pelón rubbed his stinging hand. Would he ever learn to wait before reaching for the things Santos held in his hands?

Santos moved with the rhythm of waves, swaying and calling out to the spirit of smoke. His chant was transported upward by the breeze, the ancient words carried to the heavens.

Pelón, Pelón, Cabeza de Melón,
cuando eras chico te decían mojón.
Brazos de flauta, naríz de zanahoria
hay que seguir con la historia.
Estas muscular, un esuper esqueleto,
toma esto con todo respeto.
Es cigarillo de cosa buena,
las verdolagas se sirven en la sena.

Emo, emo, hay viene el supremo,
eso, eso, hay viene el congreso.
Ahora lo verás, fuera de esto, no hay más.

Pelón, Pelón, you melon head,
one of your childhood nicknames shows you wet the bed.
Arms that resemble two flutes, a nose we can call a carrot,
let us go on with the story in order to share it.
You is muscular to the max, a true super skeleton,
take this respectfully or be turned to gelatin.
It's a cigarette my friend, so good it's incredible,
verdolagas, like greens, are very edible.

Emo, Emo, with a little bit of fudge,
the translation would read here come da judge.

Eso, eso, no need to worry,
he brought his friends the hanging jury.

Now you will see and now you will know,
this is all there be, there ain't no Moe.

Later, when the other apprentices were questioning Pelón about his encounter with the mixture and the mechanical monster, Pelón sadly told them what had occurred. He shamefully reported that the spirit of the mixture must not have approved of him. It denied him superhuman strength, refusing to respond to the wishes of his will. He had to content himself with the power of the chilepuro, unable to successfully challenge the monster. He had to empty the concrete truck a wheelbarrow at a time, like any other normal being.

Pelón was a frightened soul as he prepared for sleep that night. He wondered how he would fare against the more formidable foe when he had failed so miserably that day. What would he do if the cu-cui came in the night?

PELON DROPS OUT

CHAPTER TRES

PELON DROPS OUT

Pelón did not pass the night in the restful but alert slumber of a warrior. His body kicked viciously at the covers, the disheveled sheets were a sign of his battle with the monstrous entity. He was barely able to defend himself against the faceless figure in his tormented dream. The cu-cui wore huge dark sunglasses, its features hidden behind the tinted glass.

His mother, awakened by his whimpers and moans, opened the door to his room. Her protective concern for her son prompted her to make the sign of the cross as she stood in the doorway. The dim light cast an ominous shadow over the tortured figure tossing on the bedroll.

"Ay María Purísima," she whispered. "Pelón, I told you not to eat patas de cochi with your dessert. It's your father's fault. He's the one who started you on your strange ways when he taught you to put strawberry jam on sardines," murmured Mrs. Palomares to her unhearing son who was in the throes of a nightmare.

Her soft voice entreated God to watch over his son, *mi'jo,* in the dangerous hours before dawn. In the morning she would gather the the branches of the yerba buena which grew by the water faucet in the backyard. Boiling the leaves, she would make the time-honored brew for her son. The herbs would help her foolish boy who insisted on subjecting his stomach to unimaginable tests of intestinal fortitude with her own renowned chile picóso, which had won her a prize at the yearly Chicano Chile Festival.

She closed the door softly behind her, leaving her son to fight the forces of the night. She prayed for the tormented figure who struck frantically as his dream's unfolding drama continued. She could not know of his terrifying struggle to escape the clutches of the avaricious cu-cui who chased him relentlessly across a plain of broken soda bottles and broken promises.

Drops of rain striking metallically against the screened window accompanied the fading rings of Pelón's alarm clock as he slowly lifted his eyelids in the dark room. He waited for daylight to sneak through the windows to stealthily push the night away. The morning light prodded the night's shadow westward along the walls of the warm room during the half hour in which Pelón stretched and yawned, wondering if he should sleep late or get up.

He heard the bed in his parent's room announce his mother's rising. The softly creaking springs told him his mother's knock would soon be heard at his door. The floor quietly groaned as his mother made her way to his room. The shelter's hardwood ribs pressed delicately against the structure's lungs with each slippered footsteps. Sighs from the slumbering house proceeded along his mother's path as Pelón lay thinking about the night's encounter with the cu-cui.

"Go back to bed, mom. I'll just have some chocolate and pan dulce," said Pelón when his mother came to his door. She would not have to make him lunch for there would be no work this day. He pressed his face against the cool glass of the window and studied the clouds for some indication of their plans. A misty form, a cloud disguised as a woman carrying a water-jug on her head, her face hidden by a charcoal-grey rebozo draped over her head, told Pelón it would probably rain all day.

Pelón drove around, his car splashing playfully through the streets as he felt the day prod his body with nervous energy. It sent him in search of something to do until a more reasonable hour arrived and he could visit Santos Trigeño. He did not want to disturb the maestro before eight o'clock.

Drizzly moisture engaged in arm-wrestling contests with his car's windshield wipers. The pace of the contests increased and decreased with the car's motion as Pelón drove toward a nearby canyon where there was still undeveloped land.

Stopping his vehicle on a dirt road which led to the oil fields Pelón knew were beyond the foothills, he watched as the trees and shrubs bathed. The wind scrubbed their backs and shed them of dust and dirt. The shiny faces of the manzanita and mesquite glowed their smile at Pelón. He was a visitor sitting appreciatively aside as they let the momentarily appearing sun dry behind their ears.

The shower subsided and the birds shook the water from their huddled bodies to begin singing their greeting to the sun. The sun waved back through a break in the march of water-bearers hurriedly traveling to quench the thirst of a thousand thirsty streams in the mountains.

Pelón's foot crunched a good morning to the ground, the slamming of the car door behind him temporarily interrupting a chorus of birds rehearsing on a nearby oak. The cold damp air reached out with sharp claws to gently scratch a shivery hello. Occasionally reaching to knock gleaming droplets of moisture from the glossy branches of the surrounding foliage, Pelón jogged along the access road.

Cotton-tails skidded across the road before diving into this undergrowth; furry midgets scurrying to avoid the giant's ponderous feet as Pelón's boots carried him upward along the muddy road. He made it to the top of a boulder-strewn hill overlooking part of el Cañon de las Yerbas Santas, the Canyon of Holy Herbs.

The slippery clay surface of the road made the return trip to his car a lark. Pelón slid gleefully downhill without losing his balance as the rain returned. He gracefully careened down the slope, his laughter spurting puffs of steam his fast-moving body outran—a locomotive racing madly through the verdant landscape.

Drying his face with the front of his shirt, Pelón bid a silent farewell to the cañon. Mud thudded against the car's fenders like cartwheeling fudge, the sound reminding him of bicycles with playing cards attached by clothespins to their axles, the spokes resounding as they strike against the cardboard motors kids invented to change their motorless bikes into motorcycles.

Standing outside the gate to Santos' house, Pelón hesitated before pushing the slatted door open. A cowbell tied to the steel hinge made knocking unnecessary as he stepped on to the worn wooden porch. Santos peered from the window as Pelón wiped the mud from his boots. He took turns running his boots on the edge of the smooth-planked steps, the escalones that were sculpted with messages from the feet of previous visitors.

"Tienes hambre, cuerpo de flauta," chuckled Santos as he stirred the contents of the frying pan. It was an affirmative statement, an observation by the maestro that the lean apprentice looked hungry.

"I made some scrambled eggs with pieces of fried corn tortillas and there's plenty of frijoles. My wife is gone, leaving me with strict orders to clean some more beans before she returns."

"Sit down, Pelón, I know you're hungry. That's why I don't *ask* if you want to eat. I know you were taught to refuse politely at least twice before accepting the offer to share someone's food. I know more about you than you suspect," spoke Santos with convincing authority as he walked toward the seated Pelón with the frying pan in his hands. He served him a mound of food, a serious expression on his usually smiling face.

"It is good that you say thanks to God before eating," noted Santos. He observed Pelón's silent benediction over the tasty offering to his growling stomach.

"A man knows how to thank God for everything, even when there is not enough food for everyone to share. There are spaces, intervals to the world that are the domain of man's will. The borders of this domain make up the territory where a man's faith and belief in God are most easily seen. It is the area lying between the outer limits that are important to a man of the world. The daily detail of things, encounters with people who appear not to be like yourself, for example, lay within the scope of this area where your faith is most needed. This is the area where your faith must sustain you, Pelón."

"You must be strong, with an invincible will, Pelón. That is why a little act like thanking God for your food is also an important thing. The tedious tasks and seemingly boring similarity of people and things may form a cloud of doubt fogging the atmosphere to deprive you of your hard-won clarity," instructed Santos, having seated himself at the table with his own serving.

Pelón wondered how this man, this maestro, could possess such a vocabulary and such deep insights. He knew that Santos had not gone to high school. Perhaps he was hypnotized, his mind translating an ordinary man's mundane conversation into statements of philosophy. Perhaps it was a dream, taking place in his sleep or while he was reading a book; daydreaming. A sudden jolting crunch convinced him of the reality of his surroundings as Pelón winced from the unexpected event.

"¿Qué pasó? Did I say something that struck a nerve?" inquired a puzzled Santos.

"Somebody didn't clean the beans very good. I just bit into a rock," stated Pelón reluctantly, not wishing to offend his host. He picked the bits of masticated metamorphic pebble from his mouth, hoping his braces were intact.

"Impossible," replied an incredulous Santos. He peered curiously at the napkin on which Pelón had dropped the particles.

"Somebody must be after you. Yes, that's it, somebody is trying to harm you. Think. Who could it be? Have you any enemies who might seek the help of a bruja in seeking vengeance?"

"No, I can't think of anyone," replied Pelón, his voice fading as he heard a distant cry resembling a cat. The meowing sounded like the mournful moan of a woman who has lost her children.

"¡La Llorona!" exclaimed a startled Santos. "You are indeed walking in danger. You must have more power than I thought. You puzzle me. I can't figure you out at times. How can a tapado have such luck. If you can call being called by La Llorona luck," added the impressed maestro. He wondered at the apprentice's good fortune at having the phantom lady on his trail. It was said her cry in the night could freeze a man's heart if he chanced to cross her path without the protection of a sprig of cilantro hanging from his neck.

"La Llorona," whispered Santos gravely to a perspiring Pelón who had lost his appetite. "We are going to have to take special care today. She has not been known to come during the day since the time of your grandfather. Perhaps it is the rain that brought her out. In any case, you must not leave this house until we have solved this mystery. We must know why the Crying Lady is after you."

"What must we do, maestro?" inquired the mesmerized menso of his mentor.

"Do not ask what *we* must do, my son, ask what *you* must do. I cannot help you in this matter. I can only advise. You must remain absolutely silent until I think of something. I must search my brain for a solution. Be quiet while I think," commanded Santos. His gaze moved over the room for a clue, like a flashlight in a haunted house after midnight.

"I have it!" he said with a bang on the table. "I remember my own maestro showing me how to find answers where there are no questions. Stay here while I clean off the table."

After a few minutes of activity, Santos emptied the contents of a large paper sack onto the now cleared table. A pile of pinto beans cascaded onto the flowered tablecloth before the bewildered Pelón. Santos motioned with a finger over his lips for the puzzled youth to remain silent.

"Listen and pay close attention, your life may depend on following my instructions exactly. You must clean these frijoles flawlessly. No rocks or dirt clods must be left in these beans. When you are through with this most serious task, I shall count the pieces of foreign matter and tell you the meaning behind the results of this challenge. I must not look while you do this. It would alter the power of the procedure. I will be here, washing the dishes and cleaning. We must not speak to each other. Nor can I keep my eyes on you. Quickly, do not tarry, it may be too late already."

The nervous neophyte worked feverishly, separating the beans. He placed each bean in the new pile he started when he pulled the first frijole from the pile with sweaty swiftness in search of rocks and clods. After about a half hour, Pelón locked up, his task accomplished. Anxiously, he waited for Santos to turn his head so he might signal wordlessly that he had completed the procedure.

"Ah, you did well," said Santos at last. He smiled as he surveyed the neat pile of frijoles and the much smaller stack of tiny terrones and rocks Pelón had thoughtfully placed on a napkin.

"La Llorona," whispered Santos gravely . . . .

"Let's see, how many rocks and how many terrones are there?"

"Six rocks and three terrones."

"It is good. That means you can go now. You will be safe. Go quickly now, it is best if your body is exposed to the cleansing air. But beware of the night. You have a new enemy who might unite with the cu-cui. Be of strong will, my son, you will need much power to contend with these two opponents. You are indeed lucky. Imagine, el cu-cui and La Llorona pairing up especially for you. To survive a night of their combined attack would make you a strong warrior. Go now, quickly."

"But Santos," meekly protested Pelón. "You did not tell me what the task meant. How can I learn what a warrior must know if you do not explain the meaning of the terrones and the rocks?"

Putting a comforting arm around the still frightened initiate, Santos whispered the secret into his ear.

"Nine, an odd number, means it was only a cat. The total number, a combination of six and three, means I will have to talk to Enano Crecido who owns the store. I must speak to him about the quality of beans he sold my wife."

PELON DROPS OUT

CHAPTER CUATRO

PELON DROPS OUT

Pelón, Pelón, Cabeza de Melón,
toma esto muchacho masetón.
Call to the wind, beckon the cloud,
cover your máscara with a golden shroud.
Chant on time and make it rhyme,
look in the sky for a rope to climb.
Llámale al amigo, el Louie Louie,
ask for help in your fight with the cu-cui.

Santos invoked the spirit of the mixture, his voice gratingly murmuring the words to a secret chant which would herald Pelón into the latest phase of his struggle to become a man of power, a giant among men, a tower of power. His voice fell to a whisper, the words incoherent as he hummed his ageless harmony over the metal mass he had moments before molded into a fantastic facsimile of a pipe. The smoldering mixture lay awaiting Pelón's puffs.

Pelón, Pelón, Cabeza de Melón,
buscando secretos en el terrón.
Creíste y te buscaba la mentada Llorona,
bien asustado por la fantasma gritona.
Al saber que era gata, te pusiste los huarachis,
muy alegrado, esperando los mariachis.
No te creas muy suave con ganas de bailar,
chansa que vuelva quieriéndote abrazar.

Pelón, Pelón, you melon-headed jewel,
looking for secrets using clods as a tool.
You thought you were pursued by the Phantom Lady,
scared to death, a bright day turned shady.
When you found it was a cat you wanted to dance,
very happy for another chance.

Don't get over-confident and call the mariachis,
wait a while on those platform huarachis.
Fate may call for a ladies' choice,
La Llorona may beckon with an eerie voice.

After several minutes of intense concentration, Santos
waved his hands over the smoking pipe. Opening his eyes slowly, the maestro smiled euphorically at the apprentice seated before him. Both of them sat cross-legged on the kitchen floor
where Pelón had his experience with the Llorona the previous
night.

"Do you have any questions before you smoke the mixture,
my son?" asked the somber Santos. "This is serious business,
make no bones about it. It is best if you remember the Vowels
of a Warrior, the sacred promise you made when you agreed to
make this journey today."

"Do not speak them aloud, Pelón. No one must ever hear
them. Say them to yourself. Let your silence speak to the other
world before you proceed with the next step."

"Maestro, I do have one question, if I may foolishly make
my confusion known," haltingly uttered the anticipating travel-
er. "I know that confusion is not the way of a working warrior.
You have told me many times. Clarity is the answer; truly. But I
am puzzled, master. I am afraid my question will be a foolish
one to which my muddled mind cannot find an obvious answer."

"Do not fear that your question will seem ridiculous, my
son. The folly of men is their fear of asking questions which
their pride refuses to allow them to ask. A child cannot grow
without asking about the world. Neither can a man shrink without overcoming his petty care about seeming ignorant. A man
must shrink. He must become smaller than the smallest of
creatures in order to understand the marvels of the universe.
Ask, my son. I shall do my humble best to seek an answer to
your question."

"You mean I must become as small as my brother, the moth?" inquired Pelón, temporarily forgetting the question he had in mind.

"No, the moth is not your brother. It is your primo político, related to your mother's brother-in-law on his grand-father's step-father-in-law's side of the family by virtue of being adopted," explained Santos solemnly. He was speaking to Pelón of the complex genealogy by which warriors trace their relationship to the creatures of the earth.

"Well," hesitated Pelón, still afraid to voice his original question. "You have called this thing containing the burning mixture a pipe. Yet minutes ago it was a muffler from a car which you magically shaped into an object resembling a tobacco pipe. If I am to speak to the spirit of the pipe, how should I address it? How am I to speak to it, maestro?"

"Its name is not to be spoken in front of anyone not sharing the secrets of our way, remember that. It is called . . . . . ." and here Santos hesitated, gathering himself together to utter the sound which would call the spirit of the pipe from its dark un-known.

"It is called El Mofle. It is this container which gives the secret mixture the added power lacking in the cigarette form you smoked before. Though it did not agree with you the first time, I think maybe it will take a liking to you this time. I would not allow you to venture forth on this most dangerous encounter if I did not have confidence in you, Pelón. Remember all you have learned. It will be a risky affair."

"Darkness will be upon us soon. You will have to face the cu-cui with only the power of your wits and cleverness to sus-tain you. Take deep puffs. Let the smoke enter every orifice. The special mouthpiece will prevent you from burning your lips."

Handing Pelón the large pipe which somewhat resembled a tobacco pipe mated with a trombone, the maestro watched carefully as the apprentice handled it delicately. Santos had shown him the correct ceremonial manner of holding the pipe during their preparatory talk hours earlier.

The verdolagas, oja de elote and tolondrones pa' los preguntones combined in a heady mixture. The specially cured ingredients stupified Pelón with paralyzing effects. His lungs
seemed to collapse as his body ceased normal functioning. From
far away came a thundering crescendo of sounds as the pipe
tumbled to the table. The immobilized menso was unable to
control his limbs. Darkness enveloped Pelón, the room disappearing as an impervious shield covered his consciousness.

His spirit wandered through pitch-black space which was
not space as we know it. Time and motion were absent from
this state of indescribable being and non-bean Gerónimo had
once talked about. The maestro had called it Zxuitlchatlepoztl-
quazxlaboogaloo—"Ain't-syet-land of the Warrior's Spirit."
Gerónimo explained that the Spaniards, who were unfamiliar
with the language of the Indian forefathers, had mistakenly
translated it into "Ancient Land of the Warrior's Spirit."

Slowly, an atom at a time; the universe began to take shape,
Pelón witness to its creative splendor. The stars served as bea-
cons leading him to truth and understanding. With anguish, the
youth faced himself, his life's transgressions looming before his
sorrowful soul, chastising him for haughtily dismissing the commands of his Creator. A voice surpassing the vastness of the universe spoke to the expectant apprentice in the voice of the
seven seas, telling Pelón he would have to face the monstrous
cu-cui for having failed to honor his parents. Pelón was guilty of
having defiled his mother the earth and his father the sky. He
was also guilty of lesser infractions of a different nature called
Millenium Misdemeanors.

A horrifying scream caused Pelón's heart to dislodge from
his body, torn from its roots to plummet with breath-robbing
acceleration through a bottomless abyss of fear and terrifying
darkness. The universe froze in lightless horror as he saw the
unbelievably ugly cu-cui appear without its sunglasses shielding
the contorted features. Pelón cringed, seeking to shrivel into
nothingness to escape the cu-cui.

The warrior summoned every bit of his will, assuming the
defensive pose as the gruesome ghoul grappled fiercely with

Pelón in an attempt to erase him from time's memory. The battle waged with maddening intensity for eons, Pelón being saved from the slobbery clutches of the monster as he appeared on the verge of being devoured.

"Pelón, Pelón, come out of it. My wife is on her way home." Santos commanded Pelón to emerge from the other world, shaking the stunned apprentice who slowly and painfully re-entered the world of ordinary petty concerns. Looking into Pelón's eyes to assure himself of the pupil's lucidity, Santos asked the apprentice a question.

"Well, my son, what did you learn?"

"I learned that the best defense against the cu-cui is to be a good boy, be home at the hour my mother tells me, pick up any mess I make, and mind my elders," replied the exhausted warrior.

PELON DROPS OUT

CHAPTER CINCO

PELON DROPS OUT

Pelón was up before dawn, wondering if it would rain. He was unsure about the weather. It had quit raining before noon the previous day but there was a light mist falling in the darkness outside as he poked his head out the back door to check. He would have to wait for more light before making any judgment.

If it looked like the rain would not increase. If there was a chance the sky would clear in the early morning, he would have to go to Gerónimo's house and wait for the maestro to come out of his house. It was customary for the apprentice to be ready and waiting when the master exited the house to leave for work. Pelón would drive his own car. Gerónimo hardly ever told them where they would work the next day and Pelón, each morning, would be at Santos' house, waiting for his boss.

Pelón apprehensively knocked at Gerónimo Vidrios' door, the maestro's usually vicious dog, Sacasangre, pawed at Pelón in a lapping welcome. He waited in the morning drizzle, patting the German Shepherd's head as he looked around at the surrounding fields covered with wet weeds. Gerónimo's house was located in the outskirts of La Oya, in the area known as La Tierra de los Maderistas.

There was plenty of open land in this part of La Oya. The houses were a good distance from each other. Gerónimo's brother, Cubra Vidrios, lived a hundred yards away. His other brothers lived in the main part of La Oya, near Pelón, in the more densely populated part of the colonia. Quebra, who was called Capitán Jaf Ipaf, and Escoba lived on the same block, but a house away from each other and their mother's house.

The curtain parted behind one of the kitchen windows and Pelón saw Mrs. Vidrios' sleepy face peering out into the grey morning. Seconds later she was opening the door, the quiet inside the house and her kimono suggesting to Pelón that he had interrupted her slumber. Gerónimo's wife stifled a yawn as she spoke to the nervous apprentice.

"My viejo is still asleep. He said you can't work today because it's going to rain," she said quietly, not wanting to rouse her husband who might launch a tantrum at being disturbed. Gerónimo rarely slept late and Mrs. Vidrios knew he would not like being awakened on this wet dawn when he had the opportunity to sleep as late as seven or eight o'clock. The ignorant apprentice had not had enough sense to know they could not work today.

Pelón was about to offer a whispered apology when the sonic boom of Gerónimo's shout sent the dog Sacasangre scurrying for cover beneath Pelón's car. Mrs. Vidrios shuddered and Pelón cringed as Gerónimo yelled in a voice that was sure to be heard by Cubra across the expanse of unplowed field.

"Is that Professor Backwards? I bet if I told him to go out and wet the ground to make it ready for pouring concrete, he'd be out there in the middle of a storm with a garden hose. Tell that brain of a kumquat to wait in the kitchen!" roared Gerónimo, his tirade accompanied by Sacasangre's howls as the German Shepherd protected himself against the decibels by imitating a siren. Gerónimo's voice shifted to a more subdued tone, coated with softness and humility as he addressed Ana Marana.

"Vieja, will you make some coffee for us, please? Maybe Pelón is hungry and you can make us some breakfast, huh honey?" Gerónimo spoke harmoniously, knowing better than to speak to his wife in the same manner he treated other people. She was the one person who saw completely through his demeanor and took none of his ill-treatment; quick to wield the palote if he got out of hand.

Pelón relaxed somewhat as he sat at the table, watching Mrs. Vidrios pour water into the pot and add some coffee to the long-stemmed cylinder that fit inside the pot. He stiffened as Gerónimo walked in. The mean maestro was buttoning his long-sleeve shirt and scowling at Pelón who avoided his eyes.

"Do you know that I was having a good dream when you tapped on the door like a little kid knocking at the door of a spooky house. It was such a nice dream. Santos and I were pouring patios and for once you were doing things right," recounted Gerónimo wistfully, his tone changing from its subdued account of the dream to a grating lecture as he continued.

"Pelón, I left you by yourself with a little bit of work to do yesterday at one o'clock and when I went back to check last night, you hadn't done anything. What did you do between one-thirty and three-thirty, play with the plumbers?"

"I graded out five patios and three entryways. I laid out the lumber for the patios and some sidewalk, stripped the forms from the sidewalk we poured the day before, picked up all the stakes and piled them up after pulling all the nails out of them and broke out the concrete curbing that has to be replaced," stammered Pelón, trying to control his nervousness.

He had rushed through the afternoon, working feverishly to accomplish as much as he could. Gerónimo had left him with a list of tasks that would have taken three days to do. Secretly, Pelón was proud, thinking he had done a good job.

"And what did you do the rest of the afternoon? Hell, that stuff, I could have done it in a half hour when I was your age!" grunted Gerónimo, accenting his remarks with a bang on the table. His shoulders looked to be four feet wide as he hyperventilated, gathering steam as Pelón gulped in expectation of the imminent outburst of temper.

Gerónimo's shoulders shrunk to their normal proportion, the pressure valve activated as his wife stood over him, tapping the palote on her open palm as she looked down at her now quiet husband.

"How many times have I told you not to cuss in this house? And how many times have I told you not to bang on the table? Do you want to wear this rolling pin? Do you want me to embarrass you in front of Pelón?" asked Mrs. Vidrios in a very matter of fact voice.

Gerónimo cleared his throat, fidgeting with the button on his sleeve as he evaded his wife's level gaze. He decided to ask Pelón a question and divert the apprentice's attention from the scene.

"Pelón, do you know why they call this La Tierra de los Maderistas?"

"I have heard different stories about that, maestro. My mother told me it is so named because of Mr. Corta Leña's woodpile down the road. She said it is such a big woodpile and it was here before any houses were built in this area. Then a pachuco told me that it is because the people who live here like to maderear; that the people who moved out of the main part of the colonia think themselves better than the rest and boast of their superiority. And Mr. Thomath Cathtellano, my high school Spanish teacher, once told me a different story. He said it was believed that the first family to build a home here came from Mexico during the Revolution and were followers of Francisco I. Madero."

"Oh. I wonder which is right," spoke Gerónimo, pondering Pelón's information as he sat stroking his chin. "Vieja, do you know why they call this place that name? What does the chisme auxiliary group have to say about this?" he inquired, thinking that perhaps the wives of the local maestros might know the answer. Chisme, or fact-gathering, was by and large the domain of the women who had a talent for divining the truth about things.

"Well, the story about the pachucos naming the place is nonsense. We can't take the word of anyone belonging to the plebe. You know we don't think we're any better than the common people from the colonia. It must be one of the other two reasons. I'll have to bring this up at our next mitote," stated Mrs. Vidrios as she proceeded making tortillas. It would make an interesting topic of discussion at their daily gathering to talk about the events in the community.

After a good breakfast of steak, eggs and frijoles, Gerónimo instructed Pelón to visit Santos Trigeño, saying the maestro was expecting him and had the day's lesson ready. Knowing better than to ask Gerónimo why he himself did not present the lesson, Pelón excused himself, thanking Mrs. Vidrios for the meal.

Pelón arrived at Santos' house, finding the maestro alone, reading a book. He greeted Pelón with a friendly smile, asking him to sit in the living room while he finished a chapter on Marx: From Karl to Harpo. Pelón was unfamiliar with the book.

"Pelón," began Santos, setting the book aside after a while. "We should let you write a book for Gerónimo and myself. You have enough education to put words together and I can tell by your hands that you know how to type. They are even now in the half-open position of a piano player or a secretary."

"I do know how to type, maestro," replied Pelón to the observant maestro. Like all cementeros, he had keen eyes and let no details go unnoticed. "But my hands are still cramped from gripping the pick and shovel, not to mention the sledge hammer. Gerónimo left me with enough work yesterday for a whole crew of men."

"Yes," chuckled Santos, "he wants you to begin assuming responsibility and he wants you to set high goals for yourself. That way, even if you don't accomplish all that you set out to do, you will still have done more than most people who have more narrow aspirations."

"What would the book be about, maestro? Could we write about the secrets the maestros know? Or maybe we could write a humorous book about a construction-derby with the old-timers against the apprentices," offered Pelón.

"Perhaps we should have our minds on something serious, Pelón. Maybe we should write a story about the history of our people. Do you know how Escoba got his name?"

"No, maestro, but I know that Quebra Vidrios was named by his compadre Juan Conpala, one day when Juan Conpala came to work ready to surrender his will to the cursed cruda."

Pelón began the tale of the naming of Gerónimo's older brother, recalling how Juan Conpala, suffering from a tremendous hangover, had come to name Quebra, Capitán Jaf Ipaf.

"Quebra was storming around the job, his big mustache flapping as he yelled out orders to the others. He was wearing his big leather kneepads and some over-pants with a big hat on his head. He began scolding his compadre for being late for work, his mustache fluttering in the breeze as he disciplined Juan Conpala. His compadre said Quebra looked like a commercial for a breakfast cereal, but his English isn't too good and

Captain Huff'n Puff came out sounding like Capitán Jaf Ipaf. When he wrote it on the fresh concrete, he reminded Quebra that the letter J is pronounced like an H in his native language."

"That is correct, Pelón, and the letter I is like an E. Do you know how Juan Conpala got his name?" asked Santos.

"No, maestro."

"Well, he is from Querétaro and his name was Huitmai-tonginchíc Pala. He came over to this country and I got him a job as a laborer on a concrete crew. All the finishers were gavachos and one day he was standing at the far end of a slab. The masons kept yelling for a shovelman, calling, 'one shovelman, one pala; we need a man con pala, one con pala!' "

"The other laborers, all of them from Mexico, called to him and said, 'hey, Juan Conpala, they're calling you.' "

"And how about Escoba Vidrios, how did he get his name?" asked Pelón, interested in the background the maestro was divulging.

"He is named after the first cement mason in the Vidrios family. The Vidrios have been in the concrete trade for many generations. When their great-great grandfather contracted to pour a patio for a nobleman in Mexico, he invented a method of finishing concrete which is still used today. It is the broom finish which you see used so much on sidewalks and patios. Running a broom over troweled concrete, you leave grooves or marks that aid people in walking on the concrete which tends to become slick when wet. But I am getting ahead of myself," said Santos, preparing to tell Pelón the story of Escoba's historical background.

"It was very hot in Sonora where this rich man had his estate. Quijada Vidrios had to work very fast because the hot sun was drying the concrete too quickly. Though he worked as fast as he might, he did not have time to sprinkle the gold, which the nobleman provided, onto the cement before it dried."

"The nobleman, seeing that his patio would not glitter like the sun or have the chips and dust glowing in the moonlight, angrily stomped out the door, meaning to tell Quijada Vidrios what he thought of him. He stalked out the door, through the entryway and onto the patio. The cementero watched as the nobleman walked angrily towards him, looking like a policeman chasing a long-hair for throwing rocks. Quijada watched as the nobleman slipped on the slick surface of the patio and then humbly walked over to the man and said, 'I am very sorry, señor. Let me see what I can do with this dreadful situation.' "

"Quijada went to the barn and found a steel rake. Being an ingenious man, he dragged the rake across the patio which had not completely hardened. He left grooves which would enable the nobleman to tread on the patio without fear of slipping. The nobleman was impressed and asked him where he learned this trick and what the tool was called, having never had to work with tools himself."

"Quijada explained that it was a rarely used method of finishing concrete and that he would have to charge a little extra. He told the rich man it was a broom, holding the rake proudly before him."

"Later, after Quijada had collected his payment and the rich man stored the gold dust and chips, he proceeded to the barn, intending to put the rake where he'd found it. A stableboy, seeing what had transpired, accosted Quijada, saying he was not easily fooled like the nobleman. 'Do you think we are all so dumb like the rich man. Don't you think I know what a broom looks like?' asked the stableboy. Quijada said, 'no te andes fijando en chingaderas, buddy. It is a rake when in the hands of a farmer but a broom when in the hands of a cement mason.' "

"So Quijada named a son after the broom and it was passed on?" queried Pelón.

"Precisely. The name has been passed from the second son of the second son. But some of Escoba's co-workers call him El Rastrío, the Rake; because, unlike his ancestor, he does not wait for the concrete to harden but runs the broom over the concrete when it is wet, leaving deep gouges like a rake."

"There is much to learn about our history and culture,

maestro. There is so much for a man to learn and know about the world. When will Gerónimo begin instructing me in the ways of the world?" asked Pelón, curious as to why his maestro propio, his proper master, had not assumed much responsibility in his training. Santos had so far done most of the teaching, with Gerónimo only an occasional observer.

"When the time comes, my son. You must first learn the things that I am able to introduce you to. The things he can teach you are more appropriate to other ways of acting. His name, for example, is an indication of the things he can teach you. Gerónimo is a name for a warrior. Santos, saints, tells you about my inclination. I teach more about the things in the clouds, the places where a man's mind sometimes chooses to dwell. You must first learn about the world that is high up in the clouds before you can be deemed ready to learn the things Gerónimo can teach you, such as how to crush a mountain beneath your boot or defend yourself against ten or twelve attackers with nothing more than a blink of the eyelids."

"There are any number of things that could go wrong if you had his powers and did not know how to control your temper or your actions. No, it would be dangerous for you and for the world. Gerónimo and I consulted the Chavalas Chismosas, the spirits of divination, regarding you. They said you should become a writer and tell of your people through the written word. They said your name shall be Profesor Al Revés and conferred the title of Backwards and Mentally Retarded on you."

"But I have found my name. It is . . . . ."

Pelón was cut off by Santos who quic kly placed his hand over the apprentice's mouth, a worried look on his face.

"You are not supposed to say that name! What are we to do with you if you forget the warnings we give you? That name you were about to utter is your spirit name. You must never say that name in this world."

"Come and sit in the kitchen while I prepare the mixture you will take today," instructed Santos, shaking his head at the apprentice's near-mistake.

*"Come and sit in the kitchen while I prepare the
mixture you will take today," instructed Santos . . . .*

Pelón watched as Santos gathered the ingredients, placing them on the table before the curious neophyte. Pelón began to worry as Santos donned a pair of gloves, reaching into a lead-lined box for some chile peppers that sparkled and crackled like volatile atomic matter. He placed four of them in the large mortar placed earlier on the center of the table.

With a sharp knife, Santos skinned some tunas, scraping the thorns from the prickly pears into the mortar. The skins of the tunas were discarded and the clean prickly pears were put in a bowl and stored in the refrigerator. Pelón's nervousness increased as Santos poured some Purex into a pan, dropping five prunes into the bleach to soak for three minutes. While the prunes were purified and Pelón was stupified, Santos added a few drops of nail polish remover to the contents of the mortar.

Removing the prunes from the pan, he placed them, one at a time, between his thumb and forefinger. Popping the pit into a waiting napkin, he placed the shriveled skins into the mortar. He ground the contents with a pestle, humming a melody as he worked. Adding a few chicharrones, fried pork rinds, he continued pulverizing the potent ingredients.

Pelón's eyes began to water as Santos added half an onion to the mixture. Sprinkling some blue powder onto the mashed mixture, Santos then poured an ounce or two of liquid from a pink bottle. Pelón jumped back as the mixture began sizzling loudly, sounding as though spontaneous combustion were about to occur. Santos kept humming, grinding, not noticing that the mortar was slowly dissolving before Pelón's wide-open eyes.

"Hmm, I better dilute the mixture a little," said Santos as he ceased his humming, at last noticing that granules of the mortar were crumbling into the mixture. "The chiles may have grown more powerful while in storage."

Reaching over the table, Santos grabbed a yellow bottle, shaking it for a few seconds before adding some of the liquid to the mortar. The sizzling subsided and Santos chopped a strange object resembling half a clothespin into small pieces, adding them to the contents of the mortar.

"What was that, maestro?" inquired Pelón, his eyes stinging and his body beginning to feel the urge to flee.

"Tolondrones pa' los preguntones. They will make it more palatable. Hand me that cup and the filter."

Pelón did as he was told, watching as Santos poured the mixture through the strainer into the cup. Concerned about waste, Santos placed the unliquified part of the mixture in a bowl and washed the mortar, cleaning the pestle as well.

"Go into the living room. I will clean up after you take the mixture."

Pelón walked into the living room, followed by Santos who carried the cup. Sitting in the center of the room, Santos motioned for Pelón to do the same. The maestro placed the cup before his crossed legs, closing his eyes and moving to and fro in the familiar posture preceding the ceremony. He began his chant.

> Pelón, Pelón, Cabeza de Melón,
> con esto se desaparece el tapón.
> Poco menso y tantito tapado,
> a ver si se quíta lo atrasado.
> Tanta educación, pero ya lo vez,
> tenemos que seguir al revés.
> Cu curú cu cú y ramalama ajúa,
> esto tiene carga como Kahlua.

> Pelón, Pelón, Cabeza de Melón,
> hay que aumentar tu educación.
> Sentado en el piso por falta de silla,
> vamos a ver si aguantas la mía.
> No seas burlesco, como el Piporro,
> tomátelo en serio, que venga el chorro.

> Pelón, Pelón, you melon-headed dork,
> maybe this stuff will undo the cork.

You're a trifle retarded, a bit slow in the brain,
perhaps a mental enema will unclog the drain.

You're very educated but blinded by anticipation,
we have to work backwards to the constipation.

Cu curú cu cú and a ramalamajúa,
how about Liquid Plumber mixed with Kahlua?

Santos stopped chanting, opening his eyes to look at Pelón. Despite his clothing, the maestro looked very much like an Indian medicine man as he sat before the expectant apprentice.

"I do not remember anyone ever conducting the ceremony in English. But perhaps the time has come for a change. The Chavalas Chismosas told Gerónimo and I that you have a difficult path ahead of you. You will have to write a book that tells of our people and their ways. Because the world is such that a man is not listened to if he does not have a title or impressive credentials, they have named you Profesor Al Revés. But since knowledge can sometimes be a dangerous thing, you shall have to adopt a disguise and use reverse logic at times. Should you ever have to speak in public, you will go as Typo Marx, wearing a poncho, baggy pants and a typewriter around your neck. Anytime a devious person tries to trap you by asking a question of a delicate nature, you will type out a message appropriate for the occasion. Let us proceed with the ceremony. Remember, this is serious business."

Baldy, baldy, head like a melon,
if they outlawed brains you would not be a felon.
What was it like, being in school,
why did you pack and leave like a fool?
I would not know, quitting the sixth grade,
if I had gone to college, I might have it made.
So many young people looking for truth,
taking stuff to escape from their booth.

It is easy to see and blame the world's pace,
for sending so many on an empty chase.
The young especially look for escape,
thinking themselves in the zoo like an ape.
People everywhere looking for release,
to change a reality that does not cease.

Shooby do and oakie fanoke,
the truth lies not in a cloud of smoke.
It would be funny but my oh my,
the things people take to bring them a high.
Looking for adventure in places it's not,
I once gave a fool chocolate-covered snot.

Santos paused, his eyes opening slowly as he looked some-what sadly at Pelón. Pulling a handkerchief from his pocket, he examined it. Assured of its cleanliness, the maestro covered the cup.

"Pelón, it's just not working right in English. I can feel it. Something inside, in my heart, whispers to me that this is not the time to change the traditional way of chanting. I think it is best if I do not proceed in English, it is bumping me out. Yes, that is it. Tiburón keeps me up to date on all the current slang."

"Maestro, I do not mean to correct you," said Pelón quiet-ly, not wishing to overstep the bounds of their relationship as teacher and student. "I think you mean bumming, not bump-ing."

"Well, whatever. I better go on before the mixture cools and loses some of its power. Be still now and let me go on."

Pelón, Pelón, Cabeza de Melón,
cesos de Twinkie como rolling estóne.
Hay que problema, me siento gacho,
quieriendo explicarme en idioma gavacho.
Hijo del maíz no viene la melodía,
Lo digo en inglés y se va la poesía.

Para cabar de fustrar, pues oiga hermano,
sufro de haber nacido Chicano.
Pero don't get me wrong, no soy chión,
tampoco soy esos con modo enojón.
Siendo Chicano es alguna problema,
aprendí palabras que no tienen sistema.
mi languaje es mezcla, hablo muy mocho,
Quien me entiende si no hablo pocho.

The chant finished, Santos carefully handed Pelón the cup. The maestro appeared concerned or preoccupied, his usually cheerful countenance reflecting a change to a somber mood.

"Do not drink all of it, my son. Save a little for me. Quickly now, drink a little more than half. Remember everything you have learned and do not be afraid. Stop shaking, Pelón, this won't destroy your body. It will purify your spirit and rid you of the curse of the tapado once and for all, I hope," stated Santos, wondering if this potion would cure Pelón of his constipated state of mind.

"If this doesn't do it," added Santos, "I shall have to send to my tierra for some special ingredients which are only available in my homeland. My cousin, Misterioso Mano de Picabolsa, is a great maestro and he can gather the proper herbs and medicines for me. Now take the mixture and make sure your shoelaces are tied in case you are overwhelmed by the urge to run."

Pelón was convinced the mixture would sear his flesh as he hesitated with the cup before his quivering lips. After what he had witnessed in the kitchen, he knew the liquid was equal to any acid manufactured by man. Only Santos' coaxing hands kept him from trembling and dropping the cup. The maestro gently but firmly guided the cup to his lips. Pelón closed his eyes and waited for the fire that was certain to dissolve the flesh from his bones, or possibly dissolve his body, bones and all.

"Swallow it," came Santos' patient command as Pelón held the liquid in his mouth, afraid to let it pass through his throat. "If you don't swallow, I'm going to tell the cu-cui to come and get you," softly warned the maestro.

Pelón gulped in a shudder of terror as he remembered the encounter with the cu-cui. It went down surprisingly smooth, the pleasant surprise making him forget the monster Santos had threatened to call. Pelón leaned back, resting on the floor while Santos went to the kitchen. The maestro returned, dropping two white tablets into the liquid before downing the remaining mixture in the cup. Pelón felt giddy as he tried to speak, the words seeming like syrup in his mouth as they flowed out in a colorful stream.

"What was that maestro?" came his gurgling question. He laughed as the words left his mouth, the rainbow stream of colors disappearing in a purple puff of air.

"Two aspirins. I have a terrible headache from trying to chant in English. They will not alter the power of the mixture and I can go into the other world with a clear head. I have decided to go with you, but first I will take a little vinegar. I am not a tapado like you and I shall add the vinegar to change the results slightly. Relax, it will be a few minutes before your portion of the potion takes effect. As soon as you get back from the bathroom, we can go on our trip."

"But I don't feel like going to the bathroom," came the melodic mixture of colors from Pelón's vocal cords. The words were pastel chords, a form of prismatic sounds that made him feel light and ticklish as they poured from his mouth.

"You will," affirmed Santos confidently. "Besides, weren't you taught to go to the bathroom before leaving on a long trip? Nothing worse than a person who waits until he is on the road before realizing he has to stop. There are no gas stations where we are going, Pelón. In fact, there is no gas because the mixture will take care of that. When you come back from the bathroom, you will have no gas in your system and hopefully you will not be a tapado anymore."

Santos returned from the kitchen to sit beside Pelón. He was about to cross his legs when Pelón leaped to a standing position, searching frantically for the entrance to the clearinghouse which bordered the world of today's lesson.

"It is through that door and down the hallway, my son. The

door on the right," called Santos as Pelón bounded around the
corner. He heard a loud thud, followed by a cacophony of
sounds fading as the bathroom door closed.

A few minutes later, Pelón returned, looking a little pale but
with a euphoric look on his beatific face. He sat sheepishly beside Santos, sighing as he crossed his legs in imitation of the
maestro.

"What was that crash and all the noise, Pelón?" inquired
Santos.

"I tripped on my trousers and barely had time to scramble
to my feet before the potion hit me, maestro. I did not think I
would make it in time," confessed the shame-faced apprentice.
"I feel as though the weight of my whole life has been removed."

"Good, maybe the mixture has worked and you will finally
be able to take the next big step along the path you have chosen
to pursue. Close your eyes and let your thoughts go. Release the
voices in your mind and soon we shall be called into the other
world. You will hear your spirit name and I shall hear mine."

The stillness of their closed-eye vigilance was interrupted by
a rumbling. Pelón resisted the urge to open his eyes, his senses
heightening their alertness as he cocked his ears for the expected call. The rumbling increased and Pelón felt everything
moving, shaking back and forth. The convulsions grew stronger,
more violent. He felt himself rocked in every direction, one
moment one way, the next instant in another direction.

He wanted badly to open his eyes. The quakes were rumbling loudly now, his body pitching to and fro violently. A
gigantic tremor shook Pelón and he felt himself spinning head
over heels. He was losing his sense of awareness, unable to gauge
his body's position as the spinning accelerated to a mind-dead-
ening intensity.

Pelón thought he would black out, the spinning throwing
him into a state approaching unconsciousness. Slowly, the
movement ceased and the rumbling was replaced by the chirp-
ing of birds and the whistle of the wind. The wind stopped and

the birds were quiet as Pelón kept his eyes shut and his senses tuned for whatever was to follow.

"Chopopóte, Noyernosinhija, you may both open your eyes. You are in the other world now. Open your eyes and greet the sun. Thank God for giving you safe passage through the land of the cu-cui."

Pelón opened his eyes as the mysterious melodic voice disappeared. They were in the desert, the gentle dawn casting delicate shadows over the beautiful surroundings. It was alive with alluring colors, the air carrying sparkling particles that shimmered in the caressing light of the morning sun. Pelón stood, following the example of Santos who was looking around at the area.

The maestro was looking and listening, scanning the desert below and the hills above as they stood on a low-lying plateau. Pelón studied the maestro, sensing that Santos was undergoing a deep emotional experience as the older man seemed to capture and hold each detail of the scene he was viewing.

"I have been here before, many years ago," spoke Santos at last. His voice was the wistful sound of a man experiencing the bittersweet intensity of emotion, the seriousness of the moment making him appear to be sad.

"I was young, like you, when I visited this place. I came here and was so filled with power and love of life that I ran through the desert, playing with the animals and experiencing time with a child's innocence. I ran up the mountains and along the desert floor, tireless, feeling the strength of the sun in my legs."

"Allow me an indulgence, Pelón," said Santos in a low voice conveying his deep feeling. "This is rightfully your moment. I took the mixture with the hope of returning to this place. It has been in my memory for so long, like a dream that stays with you. Here is all the beauty a man could ever imagine. A man can almost hear God talking in this place, speaking through everything that is here."

Pelón felt exhilarated, holding back the urge to run through

the desert out of deference for the maestro. It seemed that
everything beckoned, calling him to run from place to place, admiring the wilderness and its countless unique objects.

"Even now I can vividly remember the strength and vigor I
felt then. But it is in my memory, in my heart; not in my body.
I used to dream of what it might be like to live in such a place
with a wife. I had the visions of youth, imagining the peace and
contentment a person could know in such a world. Only the
years were good enough teachers to show me that my dreams
were nothing more than dreams."

"You are young, Pelón," continued Santos in his soft voice.
"Your mind is filled with a need for adventure and your body
wants action. You will one day find yourself slowing down, taking time to think about the world you live in and the destiny of
a man. Perhaps you will be lucky and find love. It is the only
thing which can keep your heart from forever dwelling in the
place of your dreams. For if your heart should remain here, you
would never know the good that is available in the world of
everyday things."

"Pelón, the things you feel at this moment, they are wonderful, filled with a fascinating uniqueness that makes everything speak to you of a rich experience. Taken all together or a
grain of sand at a time, it is a world that could forever fill you
with a love of life. What could possibly match such a state of
being in the everyday world except love? The everyday world is
changing so much. It has changed much in my own lifetime.
People no longer have time to enjoy their individual innocence."

"Perhaps only a child can answer our questions. But by the
time a child learns enough to explain things, he is no longer a
child; the innocence and wonder are gone. Childhood fades into
the past, and people do not know how to appreciate the world
by themselves. They do not know the wonder of things because
they have forgotten how to be alone with things and let them
speak."

"When a person becomes aware of himself, he finds that he

is alone, experiencing a solitude he can never change. I think that is why young people take things. They are aware of their aloneness and are looking for a way to tolerate and enjoy that solitude. They are looking for their childhood and their fantasies, when the world talked to them through the things they were experiencing as children."

"A person has to grow up in a world so vast that he can always remember how small he felt as a child. A child must have a world he can always remember as being huge, large enough for his dreams. That child must have time by itself, time to explore and wander in that huge world. Otherwise, the child is crowded by the people around him and when he grows up, he has no memory of a huge world to retreat to when he wants to dream or be by himself. He becomes bored with the everyday world, unable to see the uniqueness of things, lacking an imagination to take him on travels to his childhood."

"You had better run off and enjoy this world of beauty and leave me to my thoughts, Pelón. You can run and I shall have to be content to walk. Go on, I shall take pleasure in watching you run like a warrior," spoke Santos. His smile was sincere, freeing Pelón to excuse himself from the maestro.

"Thank you, Santos. I do feel like running," said Pelón as he jumped down the hill and ran playfully along the desert. He ran effortlessly, pausing from time to time to examine something that caught his attention. A rock, a plant, the view from a hilltop, everything filled him with joy and wonder. It was near sunset when he heard the voice calling him and Santos. He trotted back to the spot where they had first emerged into this world. Santos was waiting, sitting pensively on a boulder as Pelón arrived. Sweat glistened on the apprentice's body, his bronze color close to matching the grandeur of the setting sun as he ran up to Santos.

"Maestro, it was so neat. I saw so many things and must have covered miles today, looking at everything. It must be time for us to leave, I heard the voice calling. It said to come back to this spot."

"Yes," spoke Santos somewhat sadly, his face fixed in the direction of the glowing sunset. "I may never return to this place, but it was good nonetheless to return and see such beauty before I die."

"Before we leave, Pelón, I must tell you today's lesson. Just as the mixture pulled you away from the curse of the tapado and released you from your years of constipating thoughts, I must tell you that age is like the potion you took."

"How is that, maestro?" asked Pelón, gazing at the melancholy man.

"Just as the mixture purified you to your very bowels so you could understand the Vowels of a Warrior, getting old is the shits."

PELON DROPS OUT

CHAPTER SEIS

PELON DROPS OUT

Pelón, Pelón, Cabeza de Melón,
como los hacemos pa quedar right on?
Hay que llenar cierto lugar,
escribir palabras para llegar.
Porque este era el primer capítulo,
pero cambiamos el sitio, movimos el título.
You see mis friends, quiero su perdón,
este mensaje no tiene razón.
Sólo quiero hacer la movida,
a ver si puedo hallar la salida.
Es que la página ya estaba taipiada,
la ruca del taipwriter bien enfadada.
Como que quieres rehacer todo esto?
Sólo cambie los números y sigue con el resto.
Pero hay señora así no se hace, no no no,
los fastidiosos editores lo quieren so so so.

"Santos, are you sure I'm supposed to eat these things?"
asked Pelón as he studied the five acorn-shaped objects in his
hand. The maestro had invited Pelón to his house on Saturday
morning, explaining that his wife would not be home that day.
It would give them the opportunity to enbark on another adventure in Pelón's quest for truth and knowledge which the
apprentice had begun earlier when he first agreed to work for
Gerónimo Vidrios.

Seated at the kitchen table, Pelón had opened the cigar box
which Santos had placed before him. The amiable maestro rum-
maged through cardboard boxes of nails, old nuts and bolts and
baseball trading cards in search of the container from which
Pelón had extracted the five objects. Pelón examined the small
brown objects, noting they each had a hole at the top which
appeared to have been sealed with a clear substance.

"Yes, that is the way it has always been done," advised Santos. "Do you have tough teeth, my son? Those magic mocos
have been curing for over a year. They are hard enough to break
your teeth if you aren't careful. If you have ever eaten a jaw-

breaker candy, you shouldn't have much trouble with these. Go in the back yard and sit under the tree if you like. I will go out after a while and join you. You may want a friend close by when the effects of the magic mocos begin to take you into the other world."

"What do I do, maestro? Should I say anything before chewing them? Is there any special direction I should face? You have not mentioned these magical things to me before; I am not sure I am prepared to chew them."

"You are so full of questions, Pelón. Put your questions aside for the meantime. I will explain these things to you later. For now, remember what you have learned about being a seeker of knowledge. You must remember that you are invincible. Nothing can penetrate your shield or shatter the armor of your will. Your enemy is also your friend. Fear and doubt prevent you from acting, but once you overcome those things, your spirit will be kept from destroying itself by that very same fear that threatened to immobilize you."

"Fear is nothing more than memory. Too much memory makes you want to cling to the security of inaction. Not enough memory makes you a fool who plunges blindly into everything, with no regard for life."

"But maestro, haven't you said that nothing matters to a warrior. Isn't that what you said?"

"There is a difference, Pelón. A man, a warrior with memories, has life. Everything he remembers is a large part of his life. A fool does not realize the importance of memories. He only lives for the next moment, the next adventure. A fool does not truly know life. To know life is to know that one's past matters; it is a part of one's heart."

"You see, Pelón, a man has heart. He remembers things from his life that have touched him, that have given him feeling. But he also knows that he must not let those memories prevent him from leaping ahead into the next moment. He is not like the fool whose existence is a series of jumps into the next moment; always leaping, never pausing to feel or to remember."

"It is easy for people to mistake a fool for a magnificent warrior," continued Santos. He had seated himself at the table, nodding for Pelón to do the same when he began the instruction. Dressed in a flannel shirt and dungarees, he looked like an ordinary working man with a mestizo heritage.

"The fool's actions appear to be a thirst for life, an insatiable will to live. But it is not living. It is merely a race with death. A fool can enter a battle without question. The frenzy and excitement of the struggle are his heart. He lives continually at war, always needing the battle which swells his heart and makes him feel as though he is truly alive. But a man never truly enters the battle. A man, a warrior, always remains apart from it. His heart is solid, within him. It is not lost, left to wander aimlessly within the energy and space of the next moment as the fool is."

"When a man is dying, he is afraid to face death because he knows it is final. There are no more memories. Being a warrior, he faces death, controlling his fear. The sum of his life is displayed by his heart so that death will know it is claiming a life. When a fool faces death, he does it thinking it is another thrill, another leap into a place he has never been. He may even laugh at death. Yes, it is sometimes a strange twist of fate when a fool realizes his life has been nothing. He laughs at death, sensing that he is indeed cheating death of its due."

"But what about heaven? Isn't there something after death after all? I happen to believe that there is something after death. Our souls or our spirits will go to heaven or they will suffer eternally in hell."

"I am not sure how to explain this to you, Pelón," said Santos. His dark face looked peaceful, his eyes staring at the table as he continued. "God is entirely apart from what we have been discussing, though He is involved in every aspect of all reality. You see, I was speaking to you about what *I* know, about what it is to be a man and a warrior. I cannot talk to you about what God knows. I can only speak to you of what I believe."

"If a man dies and it is his destiny to reach heaven, he will be a part of that mystery we recognize as God. If he is a fool and it is his destiny to suffer the anguish of eternal damnation, he will be dead but will always exist as a part of the universe's energy; always a part of the next moment. He will always be becoming, never again to be."

"Death will have shattered him irrevocably; he will never again be even as much as a particle of dust. The terrible thing for such a fool is that the finality of his death will cruelly and coldly make him realize that his life was no life at all. His spirit, his soul, will exist timelessly, spinning erratically amidst a core of creation's energy that will not allow him to stop. He, or rather his spirit, will exist in a state of being that is always moving, with no system or arrangement of motion. Death will bring him darkness and it will bring him moments of memory. In other words, his spirit will almost know what life is, only to have it snatched away as his spirit tosses and turns."

"A fool's spirit will be teased for an eternity. Death will remind him of life's meaning one instant, only to plunge him into the next moment with not a hint of merciful hesitation. He will exist without ceasing to become, always wishing and longing for even a fraction of a second in which his spirit might stop and know what it is to be. *That* is hell."

"There is nothing, no one with whom that fool's spirit or soul can share this endless torture. He will know that he is aware one instant, only to have death turn around and deprive him of knowing. He will almost begin to feel that he is at last feeling, only to have death rob him of feeling by reminding him of death's overwhelming and unchangeable reality."

"Maestro, now that you have painted such a cheery picture for me, might I be excused from today's session? Perhaps it would be better if I were to undergo this lesson some other day. It is not that I am afraid so much that I feel I am not in the right frame of mind," alibied Pelón.

"Would you rather be like those foolish children who seek adventure and fantasy? There are many who pursue the path of a warrior only so long as it is fun or as long as it offers them escape from a reality they find burdensome. Would you rather have heard that you were going to see bright lights and that the flowers would turn into gypsies to entertain you? Hmpff, do not let your fears overcome you, Pelón. These little mocos won't kill you."

"They may make you crazy for a while, but I will be here to protect you," stated Santos nonchalantly. His manner was that of a child explaining something with innocent ignorance of the ramifications involved.

"Going crazy can be quite a good experience, Pelón. You can learn to appreciate what it is to be normally crazy by going really crazy. Just remember, if you hear your mind snap, you will be convinced that you are going crazy. But it is the magic mocos that will make you go crazy, remember that. I know you won't remember because if you go crazy, you will be convinced that you are actually going crazy. You will have forgotten the magic mocos."

"But perhaps you will be able to gain control from time to time, when you really need to. In that case, remembering the snap will comfort you. You will be reminded that it is not you but the magic mocos that are making you go crazy."

"You are terrifying me, maestro," confessed Pelón. "What do you mean, my mind will snap?"

"Exactly. You will hear it. It will sound like a brittle twig snapping or a piece of plastic popping. It is your mind breaking through the barrier of normal craziness to the room of the real crazies. It is like opening a door that opens with a sudden jerk. It's very simple; just a snap and you're there," said Santos with a smile and a snap of his fingers.

"Have you ever had your own mind snap, Santos?" inquired Pelón nervously.

"Oh yes, quite a few times when I was younger and looking for myself. It is really the only way that some people can know what lies deep within them. There are too many selves for you to be able to know yourself without going crazy unless you are strong enough to place all your faith in God."

"You see, being normally crazy, you have so many people's shadows over you that you cannot know your real self. From the time you are born, you have people casting their shadows over you, influencing you, changing you. By the time you are grown, you are no longer your true self. You are hidden behind many layers of shadows that the years produced. But when you are crazy, your true self is exposed; you can know what you are really like. Provided you don't stay crazy, that is. But don't worry, you won't go crazy. You have no reason to."

"People go crazy because they have a reason to or because they are not strong enough to extricate themselves from that room which they have somehow been sucked into. The world may be too much for a person to handle. He retreats to the crazy room where the world cannot bother him. Others never acquire the shadows of others and reach a point in their lives where they can no longer function among others who are normally crazy. Such people never acquired those layers of shadows which enable them to operate within a world whose inhabitants are a combination of those many shadows."

"Others that go crazy may have been exposed to too much of one shadow, too much influence from one person. This person's self is not his true self nor is he able to function in the world because he does not have the variety of shadows needed to function properly. He lacks enough layers to be considered normally crazy."

"Be not afraid, Pelón. It is clear that you are one of the most normally crazy persons around. You have always been very observant, acquiring the many shadows that you knew to be shadows. You may not know your real self, but you are aware that those shadows exist. You also know that you can only examine your self to a certain point in your life. Your memory can only take you so far in your search to examine the shadows of your youth."

"That is why I chose to give you the magic mocos today. You are ready and you know why you are doing what you do. If you were to take something like these magic mocos and did not know that they could do such things to you, you might never know your true self. You would always be confused, never knowing what was what or which of you is the real you. You might even go really crazy."

"Let us go outside now and you can eat the magic objects. They may be a totally enjoyable experience. It may be like a story or a movie. It may be like a dream of which you cannot find meaning. In that case, I will have to try and be of help in deciphering the meaning. In any event, what have you got to lose? If you go crazy, you won't know enough to regret it. I mean if you go crazy and cannot return from the room."

"But maestro, what if I hurt someone, or myself?"

"You are right, Pelón. I am a maestro but you have youth on your side. You might become violent. Perhaps we should travel to the desert for this next encounter with truth, my son. I could tie you to a tree in the backyard, but that would probably alter the effect of the mocos. Oh, it is not easy being a teacher in this modern world. People everywhere, no open land for one's spirit to play."

"That is why Gerónimo does not teach you his secrets himself. He lets me do the talking. Pelón, if we were in the desert, Gerónimo could teach you much about life, about the path a warrior walks in search of knowledge. He is indeed a powerful individual. He knows much and could show you things that would astound you no end."

Pelón had wanted to ask why Gerónimo Vidrios, his rightful maestro, did not instruct him. It was Gerónimo who had agreed to allow Pelón to become an apprentice and learn the concrete trade. It was common knowledge that the maestros knew more than how to work with concrete. They were known to possess powers that were special. Pelón knew better than to confront Gerónimo with a request to learn the power he possessed. Instead, he tried to learn the concrete trade and let the maestros instruct him in the other secrets at their convenience.

"Gerónimo's nature is too violent and physical for this reality, Pelón. He is obliged to curb his actions and play the part of a hard-working man. His spirit is hidden behind a mask that most people interpret as the face of a mean and bitter man. He has no choice. If he were to allow his true nature to show, people would be incapable of understanding him. They would see only terrible force and power."

"The world would certainly do all it could to destroy him. Rather than risk harming others or being himself harmed, Gerónimo moves through this world like a man who is holding his power in check. His temper is but a subterfuge. It keeps people away, lest they see his awesome power."

"I thought it was because he does not think me worthy that he does not instruct me himself. The only times he speaks to me is when I do something wrong, or when he is giving me orders regarding the day's work."

"Yes, but you are one of the few who did not run from him and he respects you for holding your fear in control. Had you been like so many others who back away from his temper, he would not have asked me to instruct you in the ways of a man."

"Maestro. Couldn't we go someplace for this lesson? Someplace where we don't have to see cars, houses or civilization. I will surely be taken away if I begin talking to an animal or plants around here."

"We are already there, Pelón. Look out the window," said Santos with a curious smile on his weathered face.

Pelón arose from the table, expecting to see the house next door, the ivy-covered chainlink fence that separated the house next door from Santos' dwelling in the suburban neighborhood. He looked out the window expecting to find it as it was when he had entered Santos' house.

Pelón knew that the brilliant sun rising outside could not be real. It was at least ten o'clock already. How could it be? His disbelieving eyes were focused on the sun which was rapidly becoming fully visible over the mountains.

"Maestro! Where are the other houses? There is nothing but hills and open land outside," exclaimed the surprised Pelón. "It cannot be."

"Go outside and see for yourself. Touch the ground. Smell the air. Do whatever you wish to convince yourself. When you come back inside, we can talk more about your taking the magic mocos. Go now, see for yourself. I have to start making some menudo," stated Santos, indicating he was going to prepare some tripe.

Pelón's first sensation upon walking outside onto the porch was a shiver. The air was chilly, as it was almost every dawn. The paved streets, the houses, cars; everything had disappeared. The sunlight illuminated the surroundings as Pelón stepped off the porch, still unable to believe that there were trees and brush where earlier there had been fenced yards and gardens. He stooped to grab a handful of dirt where there had been concrete sidewalk.

It was real dirt. The mesquite brush he touched was real. The brittle branch Pelón held in his hand broke as he tested it. It too was real. He ran some fifty yards to the south, stopping next to a boulder. Looking back towards Santos' house, Pelón experienced another shock.

The paint was gone. It was now a weather-beaten shack sitting on a small plateau amongst the hills. He began running along the uneven ground, circling the house. It did not change in appearance, nor did the surrounding country. Walking up to the side, he reached to touch the boards forming the sides of the house. They had no paint on them but they were nailed. The nails were made of iron, their rusty heads turned brown by the weather.

Running back into the house, Pelón stood before Santos. The furniture was gone, replaced by older furniture. The formica-topped kitchen table was now an old wooden table. Santos was seated calmly at the table, turning to face the astonished Pelón.

"Maestro, what has happened? Everything is changed. Where are we?"

"Don't get excited. Do you know if you are awake or asleep?" asked Santos pleasantly.

"The floor is gone. There is dirt where there used to be hardwood. How can this be?" queried the incredulous Pelón. "Please maestro, explain what has happened. Am I imagining all of this?"

"Perhaps. Perhaps not. Do you ever know for sure if life is not just part of your imagination? Is it not the routine of your daily existence which leads you to believe that the life you live is a real one? Do not spend too much time asking these questions. You are wasting a valuable opportunity. Instead of standing there like someone who thinks he is going crazy, you should be asking what lies in store for you today. The sun is very bright, it will be a beautiful hot day; a good day for dying."

"But maestro, I can't stop questioning such a strange affair. It is not logical. Does this mean I am going to die?"

"How should I know? Your death is not known to me. I say it is a nice day for dying because it adds drama to the day. It is how a warrior greets each day."

Pelón's attention was drawn to the sound of approaching horses. Santos did not seem to think the sounds strange. He sat with a calm smile as Pelón went to the window to look outside. Pelón could see these horsemen, dark-skinned men with long hair.

"Maestro, there are Indians, three of them, outside!"

"Yes, I know. They have come to see you. Go outside and see what they want. Go on, do not be afraid. Don't you watch television? Surely you remember the movies in which the White man knows he must not show fear when talking to hostile Indians. Pretend, that's all you have to do. Go, see what they want."

Pelón cautiously opened the door, stepping outside to stand before the three Indians who stared at him. Their horses appeared to be nervous, shaking their heads and shuffling their feet. The Indians examined Pelón with dark-eyed stares, sizing up Pelón as if he were an opponent.

Pelón also studied the Indians. One of them was very big, bulky but not fat. The other two were of medium build. Their bodies were lean. The Indian to Pelón's right was the first to speak. He wore a bright blue cloth wrapped around his head. He had a two-inch scar on his left cheek. He spoke Spanish.

"What are you doing on this land?" he asked, his dark eyes focused coldly on Pelón who was trying not to show his nervousness.

"I am visiting a friend. He is inside," replied Pelón, trying to keep a note of authority in his voice.

"We know that. I am asking you what it is you are doing, what is your purpose for being in this land? You would not be here if Santos were not your friend. It is his friendship which allows you to be on this land without being killed on sight. This is not a place where you may trespass without paying the consequences."

"This is our last territory," continued the Indian. His eyes did not blink nor did his friends' as they stared at Pelón with no expression on their faces.

"Many years ago, we were hunted, not allowed to live on our land. Our ways could not be tolerated by others who had weapons with which to drive us into the mountains. We have no other place to go. This is where we must now live. Strangers entering this land must be prepared to live our way."

"What land is this?" inquired Pelón. "I do not know the area or even if this place exists. I would not have come if I had known it would offend anyone. I do not come to threaten, I do not even know why I am here. Santos has not explained what I am doing here or how I got here."

"But he has told you not to waste your time wondering about that mystery," said the larger of the three. "Do not persist in asking how you came to be in this land. It will do you no good. We do not know ourselves. We only know that this land is a place where we can be ourselves, where we can live on our terms and survive on the basis of our ability to deal with the land."

"Is this land real or imaginary?" asked Pelón.

"Let us play a game," offered the third Indian. "Maybe it

will answer your question. We will tie your feet and drag you over the cactus. If this is all in your imagination, you can have much fun and laugh at the thorns."

"That does not sound like a very good game. I will assume that this is all real. Are you Indians?"

"Yes, but that does not mean anything. You are Indian too."

"No, I am a Chicano," replied Pelón.

"If you were not Indian, you would have been killed instantly by the mere act of stepping on this land. You do not know what it means to be an Indian. Neither do we, for that matter. To be an Indian is perhaps to have heart. You cannot know heart, you can only feel it. That is why we cannot say that we know what it is to be an Indian."

The three men did not shift their gaze from Pelón. They sat patiently on their horses, watching Pelón transfixedly through dark eyes. The Indian with the scar spoke.

"If you like, you can come with us. We will show you more of this land. We can talk."

"Yes, I will go with you," answered Pelón, trying not to sound too eager as he imagined the adventures lying in store for him with the Indians. He moved closer to the mounted trio, expecting to ride double with one of them.

"Wait," said the bigger Indian. "You would go with us without asking Santos for permission or advising him of your departure? That is not good. You are not without obligations, even in this place. Go back inside and talk to your maestro."

Pelón turned to do as he was told, surprised by the Indian's words. Wasn't he ever going to do anything right? He recalled his earlier mistakes which had met with disfavor when he first began his apprenticeship. It was a puzzled Pelón who turned the knob of Santos' front door. It was an even more bewildered Pelón who walked in the house, a house whose interior was once more in its original form. He blinked rapidly, examining the room which once more had a hardwood floor and more modern furniture than the house of his daydream.

*"Many years ago, we were hunted, not allowed
to live on our land."*

Opening the front door again, Pelón stepped out on the front porch as a car drove by on the street. Shrugging his shoulders resolutely, he turned, making his way through the living room into the kitchen. Santos was busily cutting menudo. The large piece of tripe was draped over a chopping board, taking up nearly half the table. A small pile of already cut menudo formed a small pyramid of honey-combed cow's stomach on the butcher paper Santos had thoughtfully placed over his wife's favorite tablecloth.

Santos worked with the skill of a neurosurgeon, cutting the menudo into strips before artfully slicing the strips into small squares. The menudo had to be proportioned so as to be accommodated by the average size throat, lest somebody neglect to chew properly and choke on the somewhat rubbery tripe.

"Maestro, a curious thing just happened," spoke Pelón.

"Yes, I know," said Santos without looking up from his surgery or allowing Pelón to continue. Pelón was about to explain the strange turn of events, his excited voice stilled by the maestro's seemingly extrasensory ability to anticipate his remarks.

"My son," began the mild-mannered maestro, his voice the epitome of patience. "Do you not remember the lesson from your encounter with the cu-cui? Have you so soon forgotten your pledge to be a good son, in order that you might avoid having to face the terrible monster. Do you not see that this is a similar situation?"

"Maestro, I do remember. I know that the only way to protect myself from the cu-cui is to mind my mother and father. But what has that to do with the disappearance of the Indians?" inquired the confused apprentice with all the humility of a struggling initiate. He bowed his head dejectedly, depressed at being unable to fathom the intricacies of this strange world Gerónimo and Santos were guiding him to.

"Gerónimo Vidrios does not call you Pelón, Cabeza de Melón for nothing. He does not call you Professor Backwards so that you may laugh at his humor. No indeed, my son, they are not meant as purely comical names. They are not, how do you say, off-the-wall."

"It is because you forget so easily. You overlook so many things," lectured Santos without missing a stroke of the knife as he cut the menudo. "All it takes is a little temptation, a little chance for some fun and adventure and phtt, you take off without so much as a look over your shoulder to wink goodbye to the people who think so much of you."

"I'm sorry, maestro. Please, tell me what I've done wrong so I can correct myself. I want to be a warrior; a good one. Forgive me," came Pelón's soft plea as he stood dejectedly before the gently lecturing Santos Trigeño.

"Forget it. A warrior does not let petty concerns weigh him down. You must gain knowledge from the things that you do, so that your subsequent actions will be tempered by what you have learned. Then you can proceed along the proper path with a firmer step. Perhaps the Indians will return and you can again have a chance to embark on an important experience. Providing you remember not to let the opportunity slip by your over-eager hands, you may have another chance. How would I do if I tried to cut this menudo and get it ready for cooking without taking my time? I would probably cut my finger off with this sharp knife in my hurry to do the job."

"Now, are you ready for the magic mocos?" asked Santos, laying the knife aside as he turned to the apprentice. "Is your spirit prepared for the occasion? You must decide. If you are ready, they are there, in the box where I replaced them when you went outside," spoke Santos, motioning to the cigar box on the kitchen counter.

"I am still not sure, maestro. My mind is not clear as to what it is I did wrong in my meeting with the Indians. I cannot eat the magic objects if my mind is preoccupied with that. Could you not help me, maestro? Tell me what it is I have done wrong so I can put my mind at ease," begged Pelón.

"It is very simple. So simple that you overlooked it. Only good people are offered the opportunity to visit their land. You showed you weren't ready when you forgot to ask permission before agreeing to go. Even though I am not your father, I am your elder and you have an obligation to me. Suppose you had gone and never returned? Your parents would have held me responsible. It is the old way, the traditional way.''

"I understand," stated Pelón humbly, remembering the ways of his Mexican grandparents who insisted on respect and proper conduct, no matter how old you were. They would have been aghast at the behavior of contemporary youths who failed to obey their parents. They would have been mortified with the current lack of discipline in families.

"I am ready, maestro," said Pelón with resolve. He reached for the cigar box, opening the lid to remove the five acorn-shaped objects. Santos cleared his throat loudly, as if to remind Pelón of something. Pelón realized he was about to make an-other mistake and closed the lid quickly, turning to hand the box to the smiling Santos.

Santos left his work at the table to stand next to Pelón. He was happy that the apprentice was making some progress and had responded to his throat-clearing hint. He remembered just in time that each session with a new cosa mística was preceded by a ceremony.

Santos ceremoniously reached for the box, holding it with upward facing palms as he squatted to begin the chant. He waited until Pelón was seated cross-legged on the floor beside him before beginning. As in the rituals Pelón experienced earlier in his training, the chant began with Santos closing his eyes and swaying to the rhythm of his high-pitched humming.

> Pelón, Pelón, Cabeza de Melón,
> nunca he visto tal mensorón.
> Cesos de queso, mente de hueso,
> te busca La Llorona para darte un beso.
> Aquí en mis manos está la verdad,
> tóma los mocos en seriedad.
> Chui, chui, coco y bop,
> al llegar al Nahuatl, hay que estóp.

Santos' chant charged the air with suspense as he terminated the first step in the ritual, calling to the spirits of the ethereal world belonging to the true warrior. His body rocked to and fro, lips tightly pursed as he nasally invoked the power of the magic mocos. His breath filtered mistily through his nostrils as he blessed the mocos in a closed-mouth supplication to their powerful spirit.

His ritual completed, Santos opened his eyes slowly, a benign look on his face as he turned to Pelón. The apprentice was once again studying the curious objects in the box. He wondered why they were not solid, why they had a hole at the top which looked as though it had been covered with a transparent substance. He figured he would have a chance to examine them closer when Santos left him alone to ingest the five objects.

"Here, put your hand out, Pelón. That's it. There are your five magic mocos. When you learn more about this business, you can pick your own. But for now, you will take these. They are very good because they came from a wonderful source. They were given to me by a great maestro, better at picking mocos than even Gerónimo. Yes, Narizón del Dedolargo was one of the late great sources for magic mocos. Some day I will tell you about some of the extraordinary things he did. They will astound you, *guaranteed*" spoke Santos, slapping his knee heartily as he emphasized that Pelón would enjoy hearing about the great man's deeds.

"Go ahead, put one in your mouth and start chewing, Pelón," urged Santos as he noticed Pelón's hesitance. The curious initiate was trying to peer into the magic objects, closing one eye and focusing the other on the tiny hole as he held it up to the light.

"My son, they are not telescopes. There are no cartoons showing inside," counseled the patient Santos, his voice not rising above its usual mellowness. "I hope you are not like those foolish children who take the chocolate off the cherry cordials so they can get to the cherry. Are you perhaps one of those who trims the crust off his sandwich? Are you so confident that you would take the more potent ingredient in the center and throw away the wrapping?"

"Oh no, maestro. I was only wondering about this hole; see? It looks as though they have been sealed over."

"Nonsense. It is the way they are. We do not tamper with the magic mocos, although I have heard that the hippies have created a synthetic copy of these magical objects. Will they ever learn? But never mind, we mustn't let my concern cast a cloud over your day. Go ahead, chew the first one well. I will get back to my menudo while you eat the five objects. I will also prepare some chilepuro. You can have some later to give you strength."

Santos did not use his hands to rise from his squat position. He seemed to float upward, his legs straightening as he reached sufficient altitude to stand upright. His launching was announced by the staccato drumbeat of the Sphincter Drum and Bugle Corps as the fumes from his solid-fuel propellant filled the kitchen. Pelón fought for his breath as the noxious vapor enveloped the room, overwhelmed by the odor which took the starch out of the curtains. Mrs. Trigeño had only that day hung the freshly ironed cloth on the metal runners over the windows.

"Fuchila," sighed Santos, his face wrinkled in sourness as the acrid odor permeated the room. He quickly threw a limpiador, a large cloth, over the menudo, protecting it from the fall-out before opening a window.

"I must speak to Enano Crecido about those beans he sells. I am beginning to suspect they have some foreign substance in them. But perhaps I speak to hastily. It may have been the food I had sent over from Taco Flaco."

Pelón could not hear the maestro, the uneaten mocos lying at his side where they landed when he hit the floor in a swoon. His eyes were open but he could see nothing but a bright light. His ears were tingling as a fierce buzzing noise filled the room. He was conscious, yet unable to move a muscle as he lay immobile, victim of the putrid power of Santos' nasty gymnastics.

The light turned into a rainbow, the buzzing became the chirp of a meadowlark as fresh air found its way to the stricken Pelón. His eyesight returned, enabling him to see the embarrassed Santos who was opening the back door to augment the flow of air provided by the two recently raised windows.

"I am sorry, Pelón. It was unpardonable of me to forget that you do not know all of our ways as yet. You have not learned to protect yourself against many of our strategic weapons. You are strong, though, and you recovered very quickly," observed the maestro, carefully scrutinizing Pelón for any signs of permanent damage.

Pelón fondled his nose, pushing and prodding until a semblance of feeling returned. It was the last part of his body to recover from the creeping attack which had felled the still somewhat woozy warrior. It stood to reason, being the first part of his body to feel the effects of the vaporous knife cutting him off from consciousness.

"How do you feel? Are you okay?" asked the concerned Santos.

Pelón replied affirmatively, though he still felt a little weak as he remembered the devastating mist which had choked the consciousness from him so unmercifully.

"Hmm, that gives me an idea. Perhaps I should show you one of the most formidable weapons in a warrior's arsenal, my son. Yes, I believe now would be a good time. You have proved to be strong and your recuperative powers are impressive. Put the magic mocos back in the box and set it aside so I can show you this tactic. Stand there, in the middle of the room. Don't be afraid, I will not give you the full treatment; just a small sample."

"No, maestro, I do not feel well. Perhaps another day," came Pelón's plea as he struggled to hide his fear, wanting to run. It was all he could do to keep from cringing as Santos began a series of strange movements which Pelón was to learn constituted the proper way to execute the movida sobacutus potentus.

Santos assumed the pose serving as a preliminary to the actual execution; crossing his right foot over his outward-pointing left, his knees bent slightly as his curiously contortioned right hand pointed upward. His left hand moved deftly under his arm, cradling his right elbow to point it at the ceiling. Peering at the perplexed Pelón through the crook in his arm, his

chin resting on his upper chest, Santos exhaled with a quick
burst, the Right Guard executing a perfect trap-block on the
dumbfounded initiate.

The faint gust of breath was enough to give the apprentice a
hint of its mind-boggling potential as he staggered momentarily.
Santos relaxed, assuming a normal stance while Pelón gathered
his wits about him. Pelón shook his head, concentrating with
determined effort to keep from toppling to the floor again. He
could but imagine the effects of the martial-art movida were
Santos not the considerate person that he was. Had Santos not
bathed earlier, had he failed to apply deodorant, it would surely
have been impossible to avoid succumbing to the wild weapon.

"Oh maestro, you have completely scared me out of my
mind," gasped Pelón. "You could ruin someone with that movida. I cannot practice such a crude and dangerous way of overcoming an opponent. It is such a dirty way of fighting. I would
be ashamed to use it, especially in public. I certainly would not
want my mother to know I was such a person, maestro."

"I understand your reluctance, my son. But in a matter of
life and death, in a struggle, you must call upon all manner of
protection and the sobaco is no more an obscene weapon than
anything else when it comes to fighting," explained Santos, knowing that underarm odor could be used by a warrior without
need for shame.

"My son, you must remember that we are not stationary
beings that exist within one portion of time or within one dimension of the space that is our life," began Santos, measuring
his words as he spoke. The apprentice had much to learn about
what is proper and what is improper for a warrior.

"We fluctuate, go back and forth, between many moments
which have within them the parts of our life in one portion or
another. Sometimes we are within a moment that contains very
personal elements, emotional projections of our mind that have
the past, the present and our dreams for the future within them,
existing within the boundaries of that moment. Sometimes the
moment is a questioning one. Many things within and around us

stimulate us to wondering, asking silently for answers to the questions that go on in our minds."

"Other times, we are caught up in the moment of others, riding along on their momentum, reacting to their behavior. We may be so busy reacting, being a social person, that we do not truly have time to capture the moment for ourselves so that we may know what we are making of that part of time. There are all manner of moments, combinations that are manifold. But you will learn to see the similarities so that one day you can be in the center of all moments, whether they are solitary or social. Then you will have reached that point where you can understand that in the struggle, as in everything else, all things are equally meaningless in their significant particular meaning. In other words Pelón, todo tiene valor en la batalla."

Pelón considered Santos' words, pondering the meaning of Santos' last words which meant, everything has its worth in the struggle, or, in a struggle, nothing is unheroic.

"Put the magic mocos away and out of your mind for a while. They will have to wait for another day. I must finish preparing the menudo so it can be ready for tomorrow when the cursed cruda is expected to pay me a visit. The cu-cui and La Llorona haunt boys and foolish men, but the cruda, that is reserved for the biggest fools of all. Only the menudo sprinkled with bits of onion, cilantro, lemon, and containing a lucky foot can ward off the terrible effects of the cruda."

"But you do not have to be suffering an attack of hangover to enjoy menudo," piped in Pelón, hoping Santos would invite him for Sunday breakfast of tripe and hominy. He had stopped on his way to Santos' house, purchasing two patas de rez which the maestro had asked him to select carefully from the meat counter in Enano Crecido's store."

Santos had warned Pelón to make sure he was buying cow feet and not some other animal's. He reminded Pelón of the sly storekeeper's sale of used tennis shoes to unsuspecting patrons who were convinced by the fast-talking Mr. Crecido that they were buying feet from the fleet-footed and rarely seen vaca de

Huahaca. The impressed buyers were happy to pay a high price, swayed by Enano Crecido's salesmanship in describing the imported delicacy's qualities as compared to ordinary patas de rez.

"I would ask you to stay but Gerónimo and his brother are due to arrive soon for a preparatory session. My wife won't be home tonight. It will give us the opportunity to practice some of our old rituals while we drink the liquid from the maguey plant which will bring the cruda to its culmination. You are too young and have insufficient power to deal with it as yet, Pelón. You do not know how to prepare for the cruda, nor how to mascar la masa as we do in our mitote."

"But maestro, I can drink tequila and chew the fat. I would like very much to stay so I can listen to your stories. I promise not to get in the way or interrupt," stated Pelón, his eagerness momentarily casting humility aside as he begged to be included in their session.

"No, this is for older men only. You have better things to do on a Saturday night. Besides, you think you can keep up with Gerónimo's brother, Capitán Jaf Ipaf. Hmpff, you are stuffing sand in my tamales if you would have me believe you could sit at the same table with such a man. Capitán Jaf Ipaf has had more tequila run off his mustache than you will ever put in that jelly belly of yours, Pelón. Run along now, your mother probably needs you around the house."

"Could I stay and cut the slices of lemon for you?" pleaded Pelón, willing to act as a servant to witness the forthcoming mitote.

"Lemon? We are not drinking tea, my son. We eat whole onions with our tequila and lick gunpowder off our wrists instead of salt. Pelón, perhaps you don't realize that I am talking about real men. We are the last of a rare breed, the last of the Mojados. We only call the mixture tequila for lack of a better name. Actually, it is a combination of liquified sterno, tincture of TNT, distilled dynamite, pulverized Cobra teeth and the squeezings from centipede socks. We only call it tequila so the neighbors won't think we are strange. Would you like to stay and drink with us?"

"No, thank you anyway, maestro," spoke Pelón, cradling his stomach as he exited the maestro's house imagining the potency of the concoction Santos had mentioned.

PELON DROPS OUT

CHAPTER SIETE

PELON DROPS OUT

The sunset was so beautiful, casting a glow that changed the surroundings. Vibrant hues of color reached out to touch the buildings in the apartment complex. Pelón was seated on an upside down wheelbarrow, Santos and Gerónimo to either side of him as he watched the hypnotic hand of the sun reach out to mold the scene with its orange and purple fingers. The red palm of the sun moved slowly towards the horizon, the tantalizing movements of its deep-colored digits changing the forms and shadows into a silken portrait luring Pelón's mind into another world.

Resting after a hard day of pouring patios and sidewalk in the apartment complex, Pelón stared ahead, forgetting the maestros momentarily as he let himself merge with the softly alluring scenery. Perhaps it was the strenuous labor which stilled his usually active brain, allowing him to feel the air as it became charged with irridescent particles. It seemed as though the sun's hand waved caressingly over the world, bringing a soft breeze to life as Pelón watched and felt.

Life stood before him, captured in the grandeur offered by the receding sun. There were no voices in his mind, no questions or images; only the scene before his alert eyes as he felt the earth sigh a welcome to the cool evening. It, too, was grateful for a respite from the hot summer's rays.

"Now is a good time to speak, my son," came Santos' soothing voice. He and Gerónimo leaned against two low planters the bricklayers had completed only that day. They looked tired, yet their eyes spoke of energy and life-force, conveying the message of those who labor daily and feel the earth thanking them for their work by granting them the vision of a peaceful sunset.

"Give words to what you feel at such a moment as now, and you will be as the eagle who sits atop the highest mountain witnessing the world below. Express what your body is experiencing at this wonderful time and you will be as the smallest creature looking up from the deepest canyon at the sky above. Do not think of what your words mean in terms of your personal self. Do not stop to listen to your words in hopes of re-membering what you feel. Let yourself echo what the world around you is saying."

Santos' voice coaxed Pelón, mesmerizing him with its lilting quality as Pelón looked out at the sunset. Without knowing how, his voice came from within, escaping Pelón's confinement to drift in the breeze.

"It cannot be, maestro. I am too much a part of myself to become a fragment of the beauty I see before me. It is so beautiful to see the world at such a time when it is like soft velvet that you can lose yourself in it like a baby happily cuddling on a bed of newly washed linen. It makes me want to cry to see such beauty and peace, yet knowing I can only hope to reach such a state of bliss for short periods of time while I live, maybe forever when I leave my body."

"Perhaps my tears are the realization that I am alone," continued Pelón, seated as he viewed the sky's evening performance with no thought of what he was saying. "I can never share such a pure state of happiness with anyone. My self is a constant reminder that I am alone with my heart, walking through a fog in hopes of entering a clearing where I will see the smiling face of a true friend. I am lonely, so lonely that I yearn to lose myself in the innocent loveliness that I see before me. The sun is spreading a final glow to remind me of the promise it offers for tomorrow. Maybe that is what keeps me from closing my self off to my spirit. Perhaps it is the memory of today and yesterday combining into a dream for tomorrow that keeps me open to life."

"I think that if I did not have the sight of the sun's good-bye, I would not wish to open my eyes to another day. I would let the world become a mist-filled valley where I would wander aimlessly until death came to relieve me of my sorrow. I would let my lonely self overshadow the landscape until I could see nothing but solitude and yearning. Surely, I would become a person whose soul was blind to the beauty of the world, a spiritless person walking a sad path, guided by unseeing eyes that mirror the darkness existing within. My tired body would only keep going so long as there was hope of escaping the melancholy darkness by searching for a smile."

Pelón's haunting delivery was interrupted by the buzz-saw snores of Gerónimo who sounded like he was eating the brick planter. The grunts and groans of his straining motor seemed to be announcing the felling of a giant Redwood. The snores ceased, stopping when Santos nudged him with an elbow. Gerónimo was startled into wakefulness, assuming an attentive pose as he opened his eyes wide to stare at Pelón.

"I was listening. I just closed my eyes for a minute to concentrate on what you were saying," explained the maestro. "Go on, go on, you remind me of a butcher I once saw slicing minced ham and wrapping each slice individually as the hungry customer stood drooling in front of the counter. I just love the way you slice up the baloney."

"Gerónimo means to say that your poetic words lulled him into slumber," comforted Santos with a reassuring smile. "As you know, Gerónimo is a man of few words and much action. You must not let his remarks discourage you from expressing your thoughts, my son."

"Give him the magic mocos and let's see what he has to say," teased Gerónimo. "If I wanted to hear him talk like Professor Backwards, I'd stick a quarter in his voice box and stand back for a long-playing album. I would hate to see what would happen if we cut up an encyclopedia and put it in his soup."

"Did I ever tell you about the time my brother Capitán Jaf Ipaf had to give a speech at a meeting of the union bigshots?" asked Gerónimo, sitting up with a curious smile on his face as he prepared to tell Pelón the story.

"He was all dressed up in his new suit, rehearsing the speech he had paid a high school teacher friend of his to write. It was a glorious speech, the kind the real smart people give at banquets and political rallies. Somebody knocked at the door and he put the copy of the speech on the table while he went to see who it was. When he got back from answering the door, his pet giant moth had eaten all the paper and was sitting there with a contented smile, picking its teeth with a lock from Capitán Jaf Ipaf's mustache. My brother got so mad his handlebar mustache drooped into a Fu-Manchu and his eyes narrowed. His big eyes narrowed until there were nothing but tiny slits with armor-piercing rays coming out like spotlights in a dark alley searching for a burglar. Yessir, he was so mad he melted his wife's favorite praying candle and it dripped all over that moth, making a real nice decoration."

"Pues, anyway, there he was, caught in a predicament. He called the teacher but the man didn't have any more copies. Capitán Jaf Ipaf had to leave school in the seventh grade and he was afraid to get up in front of those bigshots and talk off the top of his head. He knew he couldn't remember enough of the speech to get up on stage and fake it."

"What did he do, maestro?" inquired Pelón, his head cocked to one side as he peered at the serious-faced Gerónimo.

"Well, he walked around the house, pacing back and forth, wracking his brain for a solution. He even called his wife at her sister's house where she was visiting, but she didn't know what he could so. Luckily, his big stomach helped him out. He walked around the house for about a half hour and pretty soon his stomach started growling because he hadn't eaten. He wanted to save his appetite for the union dinner because they were serving filet mignon."

"His stomach was growling so loud, he couldn't think straight," spoke Gerónimo, accenting his voice so as to convey the drama of Capitán Jaf Ipaf's predicament. "He turned on the radio, hoping the music would keep his mind off his noisy stomach and help him think of a way out of his trouble. It was a stroke of genius. As soon as the first commercial came on the radio, Capitán Jaf Ipaf knew what to do."

"What was that, maestro?" asked Pelón anxiously, wishing Gerónimo would finish the story. Santos smiled patiently, having heard a variation of the story from Gerónimo's other brother, Escoba Vidrios.

"Well, the announcer was one of those fast-talking and per-
suasive guys and Capitán Jaf Ipaf remembered he had a record
of Franklin D. Roosevelt's greatest speeches. So he cut the
record into little pieces and fried them, mixed in with a few
eggs, bell peppers, some chile and onions. He hated to miss the
filet mignon, but when he got to the union dinner, he kept his
mouth shut until it was time for his speech. Do you know that
his talk had the men standing up and applauding for a half hour
after he finished? Why, two weeks later he was elected Business
Agent and didn't have to be out in the field working like a
dog."

"He was really lucky that he mixed everything just right in
the frying pan. Those words came out making so much sense,
sounding so inspirational about the working man in America.
The men thought he was the greatest thing they'd ever heard,
until the next time they asked him to speak. After that speech,
he was lucky they didn't kick him out of the union."

"What happened, did he give the same speech again?"
quizzed Pelón.

"No. He didn't have any more albums of F.D.R.'s speeches
so he chopped up an eight-track tape his son had recorded. But
what he didn't know was that his son forgot to change the label
on the tape when he erased the speeches and recorded a party
album. Poor old Capitán Jaf Ipaf fixed it up and ate it. He went
to the dinner, keeping his mouth shut until it was time for his
speech. Then he got up on stage and opened his yapper. Every
time he opened his mouth, a nasty joke came out. All those
women in the audience, pobre de mi hermano. He couldn't even
apologize without making things worse. He had to leave through
the back door."

"That sounds a little far-fetched, maestro. I think you must
be kidding," said Pelón, keeping his eye on Gerónimo and alert-
ly awaiting the unpredictable maestro's response.

"Hmpff, that ain't nothing. He was so upset that he ran a
red light on his way home, right in front of a cop. He almost got
taken in and locked up until he gave up trying to explain and

just kept his mouth shut. Signed the ticket without a word and went straight home to let the recipe wear off."

"Look, Pelón, the sun is almost gone," spoke Santos, nodding in the direction of the horizon. "It is the best time for you to take the mocos. Sit here, in front of me."

Reaching into his shirt after unbuttoning the two buttons above his belt, Santos removed a handkerchief which was tied at the ends. Loosening the knots, he placed the handkerchief on the ground in front of him, the five brownish objects visible in the dim light before the sun slipped below the foothills. Santos waved his hands over the mocos, his eyes closing as he began his raspy chant.

> Pelón, Pelón, Cabeza de Melón,
> estuvieras regulár si no fueras narizón.
> Orejas de ule con cara de guante,
> donde hay muchacha que te aguante.
> Cesos de aire, poco atrasado,
> parece verdad que estás empachado.
> La vez que te ví, bien confundido,
> buscando saber del Frito Bandido.
> Te miras muy serio y un poco loco,
> más vale que búsques el misterio del moco.
>
> Pelón, Pelón, Cabeza de Melón,
> fuíste a la escuela y quedaste simplón.
> Yari yara con ruti cazooty,
> tienen sabor de tuti-fruity.
> Ojalá y a las muchachas no les de asco,
> mejor le hubiera dado vinagre con tabasco.
> No se enojén, sigan a leer,
> es fantasía, no se pongán a creer.
> Acuerdese de cuando estaba chico,
> te decían con gritos, saque el dedo.
> Hay mamá ya no me las píco,
> pero no me grites, me da mucho miedo.

It was dark when Santos finished the ritual, opening his eyes to gaze at the shadowy form of Pelón. Gathering the magic mocos, Santos began tossing them in the air, juggling them precisely with one hand. Pelón was amazed as they slowly began to glow like fireflies. Their movement, as Santos deftly tossed them up and caught them on their descent, became an illuminated geometric design as the pace increased.

Pelón sat awestruck while the objects revolved in the air, their movement becoming so rapid that they seemed not to be moving at all. It looked like a phosphorescent drawing of a molecule. The orbit of the five mocos sped beyond comprehension, causing them to seem frozen in space. Only a whirring sound which grew in intensity gave Pelón an indication that they were moving. Santos' hand seemed to vibrate, appearing to shiver as he kept the objects in rapid motion. The whirring sound was consuming Pelón, making his vision blurry as he fought to concentrate on the star-shaped pattern shining in the darkness.

The light from the juggled objects seemed to explode suddenly, the darkness disappearing in the startling brightness that equalled the magnitude of the sun. Pelón waited for the brilliance to subside, for darkness to return. Everything was as clear as it had been hours earlier, when the sun was in the sky. He could see everything, all around. The whirring noise was beginning to irritate him, making him shake his head to rid himself of the bothersome vibrations. He remembered an airline stewardess instructing him to open his mouth as if to yawn when the altitude forced pressure to build in his head. He decided to try that maneuver in hopes of alleviating the effects of the whirring sound.

Pelón plugged his ears with his fingers and spread his jaws wide, hoping to relieve the buzzing sensation. Santos moved his wrist slightly and the trajectory of the orbitting mocos instantaneously altered course. Each of the five objects assumed a new trajectory, their parabola culminating perfectly in Pelón's mouth. The surprised apprentice gulped in shock as the mocos rebounded off the back of his throat. He swallowed the mocos before realizing what he had done.

The tuti-fruity covering only slightly sweetened the horrible tasting objects. Pelón grimaced, feeling his stomach convulse from the sudden entry of the foul-tasting mocos. His mouth felt as though he had eaten unripe persimmons or gargled with an astringent. His palpitating pansa barely managed to resist the temptation to activate the bilge pumps. His sinking stomach donned a life preserver, panic threatening to cause the crew to jettison the load in hopes the ship would not go under. Vital body fluids were hastily diverted to the scene of the catastrophe, the pancreas pressed into service to save the survivors who were bobbing desperately on a sea of fiercely cascading foul fluids poisoned by the alien objects.

"You better not throw the gum!" came Gerónimo's stern warning.

His fierce voice scared Pelón, the maestro's admonishment causing Pelón to swallow the terrible lump which was making its way up his throat. It fell back down, descending to strike the disaster area; splashing in the pit of his pansa with results that caused Pelón's eyes to roll.

"Hay María Purísima," groaned the suffering apprentice, falling on his side as he hugged his abdominal region to contain the impending cataclysm which was sure to blow a hole in his lower thorax region.

"Have mercy," came Pelón's incoherent plea as he rolled his body into a ball, bringing his knees up to help hold in the atomic devastation erupting in his stomach. He could not recall feeling so horrible since he was a child, spreading what he thought to be butter on some warm tortillas. The Turtle Wax had been bad, but nothing could match the magic mocos.

"It is almost time. Soon another lesson will unfold for you, my son," spoke Santos with reassuring calm. He rubbed Pelón's stomach, coaxing the tenseness out of his muscles. Pelón's body was locked in a rigid fetal position, his moans muffled by his arm as he cradled himself.

The orbit of the five mocos sped beyond comprehension, causing them to seem frozen in space.

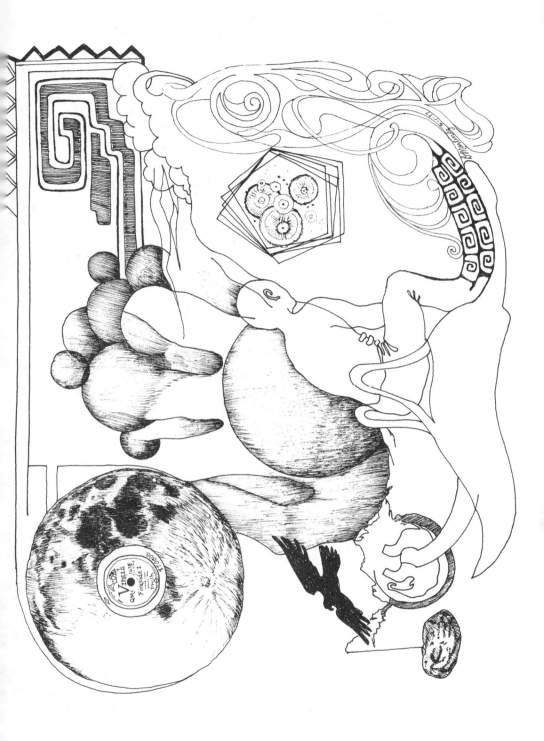

Pelón could see nothing but a greenish mist which changed to a bright red from time to time. Almost imperceptibly, a dark spot appeared in the center of the pea-colored fog, growing in size until it drew his attention. It grew until it was a line cutting the green glow in half, about one-eighth as wide as the total panorama. He forgot his aching stomach as he noticed a more natural-looking light at the top of the dark strip. If he did not know better, he would say it was as though someone were opening a zipper and soon he would be able to see on the other side. The whirring faded and he heard a hissing sound, like a vacuum can being opened, at the same time that the strip spread from top to bottom.

On the other side stood the man who had parted the zipper-like curtain of green, smiling kindly at the perplexed apprentice. He was tall, a thick mustache prominent on his tanned face. It was his grandfather.

"Vente Pelón, para que veas tu tierra," beckoned his Papá Ricardo, inviting Pelón to visit the land of his ancestors. Curiously, Pelón remembered his grandfather had refused to speak English, though he lived in the United States for over forty years prior to his death and knew the language.

Papá Ricardo talked to Pelón for a long time in that hot desert of his people. Pelón sat rapturously, his grandfather's words as profound as any philosopher's. When it was almost time for them to part, his tall grandfather said they should enjoy a moment of silence before returning to their respective realities. He would return to the land of spirits and Pelón to the other world.

Pelón sat quietly, admiring his grandfather who had assumed the body Pelón remembered before illness struck Papá Ricardo. He was tall and lean, quiet strength mirrored in his physique. Pelón was at peace, sitting by his Papá Ricardo. Everything around him seemed to fill Pelón with subdued strength that spread a feeling of well-being through his body.

Pelón laid back, gazing at the sky for a while. His grandfather's shadow passed over him as Papá Ricardo stooped to whisper something in his ear. Pelón laughed quietly and joyfully kissed his grandfather's hand in a respectful goodbye before dozing off.

"Here, drink this, Pelón," instructed Santos as he cradled Pelón's head. The upsetting quivers in his stomach turned to a twisting nausea as he smelled the awful odor from the boot being held to his lips by the maestro. He fought to turn his head from the eye-stinging smell.

"Quit messing around and drink it!" blasted Gerónimo in a nerve shattering shout. "Hurry up so I can put my boot on and go home."

"Ay, Lusitania de los mares, what was that junk?" whined Pelón. The terrible tasting liquid, despite its horrid odor, quickly soothed his distressed stomach.

"We had to improvise, so Gerónimo picked up that patio we poured today and squeezed the water out into a bucket. Then he took the gas filter off the truck and ran the water through before boiling the cream in your hardhat. He mixed the distilled remains with a little concrete-curing oil and put it in his boot. But the real secret is in the boot because Gerónimo never wears socks. Pretty good stuff, don't you think?"

"It did the trick but I thought I would pass out from the smell. Does Gerónimo have any toenails left?" inquired Pelón cautiously.

"Never mind the jokes, tell us what you learned," grunted Gerónimo as he laced his boot.

"Did I have to take the magic mocos to find out what my grandfather whispered to me?" asked Pelón meekly, not sure how Gerónimo would respond. He was fearful of the harsh maestro.

"Perhaps not Pelón, but we had to be sure and this was the best way of teaching you a lesson," advised Santos in his mellow voice. "Tell us, what did your grandfather whisper in your ear?"

"It is kind of dumb, maestro, are you sure you want to hear it?"

"Of course we want to hear it! Thousands of people are waiting to know what you learned!" came Gerónimo's grating voice.

"He said, 'The Vowels of a Warrior must be recited and the lesson of the magic mocos remembered as the next step on the path of rightful conduct is taken. I must never take the magic mocos again because next time it may be the most terrifying experience of my life. He said I will never have to take the mocos again if I remember that: A warrior does not pick his nose or play with mocos.' "

PELON DROPS OUT

CHAPTER OCHO

PELON DROPS OUT

"Okay you apprentices, get over here. Right now!" commanded Gerónimo in an amplified version of a diesel engine.

His menacing silhouette loomed like the Atlas Tireman, blocking the sunshine from the group of apprentices playing ring-around-the-Doberman, downhill from the feared maestro. They dropped the miniature Poodle they had been using to tease the attack-dog, scrambling up the incline as the terrified Poodle scurried beneath a fence to escape from the demented Doberman.

Pelón, Bambi, Tiburón, Spanicy, Fly'nn Calabera and Cockroach left a cloud of dust behind as they leaped up the short rise of newly compacted soil. Reaching the flat area where the maestros waited, they quickly formed a semblance of a formation.

It was early morning, the squinting apprentices faced the East in anticipation as Gerónimo paced before them on the freshly graded soil. Behind him was a huge square, with two-by-fours bordering its perimeter. Santos Trigeño, Capitán Jaf Ipaf, Escoba, Cubra Vidrios and Juan Conpala stood in a group as Gerónimo addressed the youngsters.

"Gentlemens, behind me is ten thousand square feet of ground that we are going to cover with concrete. This is going to be the biggest test of your skills. You will need to remember all you have learned because the first one making a mistake will be hollowed-out and left in the concrete as a plumbing fixture."

The apprentices gulped in unison as Gerónimo glared at their wide-eyed faces. Their knees began shaking, clicking loudly as the curious Doberman crested the hill to stare curiously at the assemblage. Having undergone months of training, the Doberman barked viciously, pawing at the ground as he prepared to run at the intruder who was interrupting the morning stillness. The Doberman growled ominously, darting towards Gerónimo with a quickness that would make short work of the distance between them.

"Shet up!" growled Gerónimo, catching the attacking dog in midflight. Stuffing a fist in the dog's mouth, the maestro created an instant domesticated Doberman. Freeing the yelping Doberman, he watched the now brave Poodle take advantage of the formerly vicious dog's loss of confidence. The mercilous Poodle bit at the Doberman's legs as the cowering dog dug wildly in an effort to enlarge the hole through which the Poodle had moments before made good his own escape.

"Don't be looking over there. The lesson is over here," came Gerónimo's gruff reminder as the apprentices promptly snapped their heads in his direction. The group of maestros in the background yawned lazily as Gerónimo continued.

"Chueco Floors, Incorporated, of which I am the President, has contracted to do this job bajo el ala," he commented, indicating their newly formed company had underbid the competition. Utilizing the knowledge gained from years of experience, the unlicensed company had successfully bid for the job, undercutting the others by using cost-reducing methods that would have warmed the hearts of America's businessmen.

The bid was so low that the general contractor hadn't even disclosed it to the legitimate companies submitting their estimates. Being part Indian, the expert Gerónimo had showed the contractor how to cover the tracks expertly. Only a fluke could lead the Internal Revenue Service or the Union to their trail.

"Time is money, you know that. The trucks will be here pretty soon so get your boots on and be ready. I don't want to pay any standing time while those trucks sit around waiting on you mocosos. You have ten minutes to dump a seven-yard load and then they start charging thirty cents a minute, so get that mud on the ground and don't stand around picking your dandruff. Is that clear?" asked Gerónimo, accenting his delivery by biting a shovel-handle in half.

A short-handled shovel would better suit their needs. They didn't have any use for the extra foot or so of handle. Working in such close proximity, they could avoid injuring one another by using shorter handled shovels. You rarely see long-handled shovels on a concrete-pouring crew.

"This is the first time you will be together as a group of

apprentices. We have kept you separated during your training
for oblivious reasons. As in all learning, there comes a time
when you must compete against each other. We have to see
which one of you shall be worthy to open the gate leading to
the next step in the world of a warrior. In that place, the
Vowels of a Warrior are called constantly by the wind, urging
you on in even more difficult quests for knowledge."

Turning to the group of maestros chatting quietly behind
him, Gerónimo asked them each to say a few words before the
day's lesson unfolded. Capitán Jaf Ipaf was the first to speak,
being the eldest. He stood before the group of trainees, looking
like a padded Picador who has dismounted his horse. His baggy
overpants and faded shirt, his rubber boots and large hat, combined to make him look somewhat like an aging hockey player.
Capitán Jaf Ipaf stroked his huge mustache as he spoke.

"Each of us, as maestros, has an apprentice he has worked
long hours with. But today there will be no favorites. Do your
best, boys. You will be graded on a ten-point basis. Each of you
starts with a point, providing you can put your boots on without falling. From then on, you will be judged on your energy,
your skill with the various tools, strength and ability to . . . . ."
Capitán Jaf Ipaf hesitated before turning to the maestros for
assistance.

"Hey, how do you say, no ponerse paniquiado in English?"

Following a short conference, Cubra offered Capitán Jaf
Ipaf the proper equivalent. Capitán Jaf Ipaf resumed his talk.

"You will be judged on your ability to maintain your com-
posure. As you know, one of the most important things in being
a finisher is knowing how to keep cool. Don't get excited and
don't panic, whatever you do. If you lose control, you will
work against yourself and the ungiving concrete will take everything you have to offer without so much as a receipt."

"The final category will be your ability to . . . . ."

Once again Capitán Jaf Ipaf had to ask his fellow maestros
for assistance. He asked them to translate mascar la masa, which
more or less means one's ability to sustain a dialogue consisting

of one part humor, one part making up colorful names for people, and one part that even in English can only be described as bullshitting. A good mason must be able to mascar la masa with proficiency, as reputation and community relations are very essential to one's steady employment.

Cubra and Escoba both made short statements, turning the floor over to Juan Conpala. Though he was not a mason but a laborer, his command of the trade and his skill as a laborer enabled him to stand on par with the other maestros. He was short of stature but long on heart, admired by the youngsters for his ability to work like a man twice his size. They had learned much about steering a wheelbarrow laden with concrete from Juan Conpala. He had the fortitude of an ant in his ability to handle large loads. His English, however, was a little short of equaling his compadre, Capitán Jaf Ipaf.

"Muchachos, we no worky because we likee. We worky because necesidad," he said proudly, continuing his speech for a minute or so before yielding to Santos. It was said that Juan Conpala's English was such that even someone recently arrived from Mexico, with little or no knowledge of English, could understand him. Santos began his talk.

"My sons, the mechanical monsters will arrive shortly. The other maestros have spoken of many things and there is no need for me to add to their oratory. Close your eyes and concentrate your wills on the task at hand. I shall prepare you with the appropriate ceremonial chant. There will be only one apprentice emerging from this phase of training to enter the world of spell casting and potion preparing. Close your eyes and look at your hearts for you will need much spirit in today's test."

Santos began thumping the ground with his right foot as he closed his eyes and began the chant.

> Aquí estamos esta mañana,
> buscando vida buena y sana.
> Muchos vienen y muchos se van,
> de este grupo saldrá juan.

Que tengan fuerza y corazón,
A ver qual es el mensorón.
Chubi tubi, tu gua gua tú sí,
Que canten todos, José can you see?

Mira estos con brazos de lapiz,
les dieron camote en vez de naríz.
Con piernitas de mosca hacen el hale,
son tough, con alma que vale.
Hay, no puedo, se ponen a pujar,
pero no se dan y saben puchar.
Aunque esté bien llena la carretilla,
entregan el cemento hasta una milla.

Aprendieron secretos de pico y pala,
aunque fueron regañados con palabra mala.
Ponle, ponle, aqui no hay frenos,
cada día los hechábanos de menos.
Llegaron mensos y poco mocosos,
con lengua larga de los chismosos.
Se creían muy high-tones, la mamá de Tarzán,
como que sabían hacer sanwichis sin pan.

La la la quiere decir que ya estuvo,
de lo que pasó, es todo lo que hubo.
Ahora están, a seguir con el día,
incluyendo aquel cabeza de sandía.
Hoy escogáremos el aprendís de honor,
mucho lock y ayuda del Señor.

The closed-eye concentration of the apprentices was about
to result in a sonorous symphony as Santos unending chant
mesmerized the group. Gerónimo, beginning to suspect that
they were less than attentive, was about to call out for their
attention. Their rigid posture had slowly given way to a bent-
kneed stance, each one leaning against the other's shoulder as

Santos went on with his spontaneous spiel. Only the grumbling of an arriving concrete truck saved the dozing apprentices from a rude awakening as Gerónimo was about to blow in Tiburón's ears. Tiburón, standing at the extreme left of the group, was the key domino in the row of slumbering youths who were leaning, right shoulder to right shoulder. Spanicy, bearing the weight of his fellow apprentices, posed precariously, suspended by nothing more than a faint breeze blowing out of the South.

"Aye vienen los troques," yelled Juan Conpala, startling the apprentices just as Gerónimo was about to apply pressure to the precariously perched line.

A mad scramble resulted as the line of recruits scattered, Santos choking on the dust as he terminated his chant. All six apprentices suddenly spotted the group of rubber boots by Gerónimo's truck. Dashing wildly for the boots, they began a riotous commotion, grabbing boots and trading until they found pairs that fit. Fly'nn Calabera was the first to be outfitted with boots, being the only one who could wear the extra-extra large pair which were once used as two-man rafts for expeditions down the Snake River.

"Spanicy, you and Cockroach be chutemen. We can empty two trucks at a time. Pelón and Bambi, grab some shovels and help Tiburón and Fin-Feet shape up the mud," barked Gerónimo, shaking his head in disbelief as Fly'nn Calabera flapped around the area, his huge boots catching in the wire mesh which lay inside the square.

Juan Conpala held a hooked length of steel, ready to pull the steel reinforcing mesh up once the concrete was placed on the ground. The wire mesh had to be pulled up so it would have an equal amount of concrete above and below. Capitán Jaf Ipaf eyeballed the rodstick, holding the long two-by-four in the air as he twitched his mustache. One long strand shifted upward, allowing him to use the hair as a sighting line to determine the board's straightness.

Finding a slight curve in the rodstick, he handed one end to Santos. They each held it firmly while Gerónimo breathed hotly on it, tempering the wood to a perfect straightness. Insuring that the concrete was wet enough coming down the chute, Gerónimo nodded for the chutemen to empty their respective trucks; one inside the huge square, the other truck parked outside with its chute extending into the formed area.

Capitán Jaf Ipaf and Santos Trigeño leveled the concrete quickly, backed up by Pelón and Bambi who shovelled fiercely as the two men progressed rapidly. Noticing that Juan Conpala was involved in pulling the wire mesh, Gerónimo called for Spanicy to join him on another rodstick as Spanicy waved the empty truck away.

"You got a marking pen and some cardboard in your truck, Gerónimo?" inquired Capitán Jaf Ipaf as he observed Spanicy and the maestro rodding.

"What for?" grunted Gerónimo with a massive sweep of the rod. He leveled more concrete with one pull than the youngsters could with two or three.

"I want to make a sign and hang it on Spanicy's book pocket. It has to say, Wide Load, so the shovelmen don't get run over by those elephant cheeks and suffer a hit and rod."

Cockroach snickered, holding his hand over his mouth to halt his laugh when Capitán Jaf Ipaf twitched his mustache in his direction. Owing to tradition, the apprentices could not retort to any of the maestros comments nor profit from another apprentice's embarrassment without suffering the consequences. Which meant Cockroach was the next target.

"Oye, compadre, did I ever tell you about the time Cockroach was chuteman and he had to back a truck into a real tight place?" spoke Capitán Jaf Ipaf to Juan Conpala.

Having poured out his truck, Cockroach was watching Escoba and Cubra who were finishing the last details on the far end of the forms. They would return to help with the pour after they had nailed the stakes on the final twenty feet of the huge square.

"The truckdriver couldn't see Cockroach because they were between some garages and Cockroach kept yelling in a voice like a little girl, 'hold it, estóp.' Pretty soon the truck was almost ready to put Cockroach and the end of the chute through a building. Cockroach kept peeping like a baby chicken, 'hold it, estóp.' You could barely hear his little squeeks over the noise of the engine and Cockroach started waving his arms. But all the truckdriver could see was his hand and he thought Cockroach was signaling for him to raise the chute.''

"Lucky thing Gerónimo came along and killed the engine with one look. Cockroach was dangling from the chute, still calling, 'hold it, estop' in a voice like a choirboy.''

"Here come some more trucks, Cockroach. Show them how I taught you to yell,'' said Escoba.

The husky Cockroach, deeply tanned and barrel-chested, cupped his hands to his mouth. Inhaling deeply two or three times, he summoned every bit of air from his lungs, calling the trucks in a volume almost equal to the maestro's.

"Not too shabby, huh, Santos? It has to be done just right or the tonsils get overloaded and it comes out sounding like a yodeler with tight pants,'' observed Escoba approvingly.

Escoba tamped the concrete. Due to the shape of the iron apparatus and the contour of his belly, the maestro had to use very short strokes. The sturdy Escoba worked with machine-like precision, the steady crunch of the tamp making it seem as though the maestro was running across a field of Rice Krispies.

Cubra stood with the bullfloat at the ready, the long handle of the magnesium rectangle sticking up in the air as he waited for Escoba to tamp the mud. He was the youngest of the Vidrio brothers, a truly handsome man with features that belied his Mexican heritage. His wife had nicknamed him Robert Reforo, after a famous movie star.

Cubra's son, Ricky Rock, was absent from the group of apprentices. It was decided he would go to the mountains of Mexico to study under their cousin, El Mero Guero. There it was hoped Ricky Rock would learn the little-known secret of stopping hearts.

Pelón knew little of El Mero Guero, who had been coerced

by his wife to seek the seclusion of the Sierra Madres. Pelón asked Ana Marana for information regarding the famed man. She had allowed that the handsome man was enshrined in the Chisme Hall of Heart-throbs for his ability to freeze the pulse of any woman with but a flicker of his eyelashes.

It was a dying art; El Mero Guero having no son to pass on his secrets. After a family conference, it was decided that Ricky Rock would be sent to study under his cousin. Bambi, the younger of Cubra's sons, would stay and learn the other elements of their knowledge, in large part due to his having inherited a different genetic structure. Bambi was good-looking, but he was not a guero.

The secrets of the maestros were usually passed on within the immediate family. Cockroach, for instance, was Santos Trigeño's son. Spanicy was the eldest male in Capitán Jaf Ipaf's family. Quebra's sons, Saludamela, Apachuramela, Quincong and Zapetaquiada were formerly involved in the rigorous training. Pelón, Jr. and Fly'nn Calabera were admitted into the exclusive group through the sponsorship of Gerónimo. They had passed the test; controlling their fear enough to impress the maestro. Many had approached Gerónimo, only to flee at the first sign of his famous temper or quit after a few days of harassment and hard labor.

They were working hard, the concrete trucks arriving and departing and the crew performed the task. The service from the ready-mix plant was excellent and the trucks would arrive in pairs, staggered precisely enough to coincide with the crew's pace. For the most part, the apprentices worked without uttering a word, allowing the maestros to pass on the history of their people in their dialogues.

"Oye compadre," said Capitán Jaf Ipaf as he pulled the rod-stick with a strength threatening to break the two-by-four. "Do you know why Fly'nn Calabera's family did not come to the United States until very late."

The initiates' attention was on the massive maestro as he began the account from the tall apprentice's family history.

"It seems that the first time Ignacio Calabera tried to sneak across the border with his cousin, Arturo Alambre, they ran into a border patrol. They hid but the Immigration Officer spotted Arturo behind a bush. Ignacio peeked from behind a large nopal, watching from behind the cactus as the officer interrogated his cousin. He was hoping that Arturo would not give him away or become so nervous that the migra would suspect something."

"The Immigration man, a big Texan with mean eyes, looked in his little pocket dictionary and asked Arturo, 'dondi nacio?' Arturo played dumb and said, '¿que qué?' The officer repeated, 'dondee nacio?' "

"Arturo was becoming very nervous and the big Texan was looking meaner and meaner, but he still replied, '¿que qué?' which the Texan looked up in the book."

"Ignacio was shaking and sweating, scared to death as he watched his cousin crumble beneath the hard stare of the Texan. The big Immigration man kept getting madder and madder. Ignacio did not know how much Arturo could take without giving him away. The big man yelled at Arturo, 'You dumb Mexican, I said where was you born at? Where nacio? Dondee nacio?' "

"The migra's face turned bright red with anger and Arturo could take it no longer. Shaking nervously and stuttering with fear, Arturo pointed where Ignacio was hiding and said, 'hay primo, vale más que salgas porque éste carajo hasta sabe tu nombre.' "

"It took a long time for Ignacio to try to cross the border again. But when he returned to his home in Mistimichanca, he was quick to tell his friends that he was indeed a famous man, known even as far away as the border. He changed his name to Shawn, taking the first name of an Irish priest in their village. That is how Fly'nn came to have a name that is not Mexican."

Everything was going smoothly, the apprentices trading jobs so that each had a chance to show his ability at the different aspects of the work. Cockroach was the first to lose a point in the competition. He absent-mindedly placed his father's new trowel in the path of a concrete truck. The mangled remains were examined by the maestro's committee, Cockroach standing shame-facedly aside as they passed it from one to the other, for all to see.

Spanicy was the next to feel the pressure. Extending the bullfloat too far out, he was unable to pull it back without walking in the smoothed concrete, leaving very noticeable footprints. The maestros looked at one another, making a mental note of this mistake. Spanicy tried to divert their attention by pointing to a shapely girl he spotted in the distance.

Tiburón's blunder was such that the apprentices groaned in sympathy. Peering in the distance at the girl who was sunning herself in a scant bikini, he did not notice that he had pivoted the chute too far to the right and was pouring concrete into the top of Gerónimo's rubber boot. Tiburón turned white as Gerónimo's face glowed a bright crimson.

Bambi and Fly'nn Calabera blew it. Bambi was hunched over one end of the rod, waiting for Fly'nn Calabera to grab the other end. Fly'nn Calabera bent over, just as Bambi decided to stand up. Fly'nn Calabera, thinking Bambi had a reason for standing up, straightened up just as Bambi was bending over. They were at opposite ends of the rodstick, bobbing up and down for a while until Gerónimo noticed their lack of coordination.

"Bambi! You stay down long enough for Fly'nn Calabera to bend over," he yelled.

"What did you say?" asked Bambi, standing up to address the maestro just as Fly'nn Calabera was bending over.

"Hijo de la madrugada," sighed Gerónimo hopelessly as the two apprentices resumed bending and straightening like a rocker-arm assembly on the valve train of an engine.

The pour was completed and Pelón expected Gerónimo to have them unload the troweling machines from the back of Capitán Jaf Ipaf's truck. There were two of them and Pelón figured they would soon be needed on the slab which was becoming hard. Gerónimo came walking up to the group of apprentices, holding the mashed remnants of Santos' trowel as he spoke to the assemblage.

"We are not going to use the machines. Instead, *you* will finish the whole slab. The best one will get this trophy," he announced, holding the formless trowel in the air. With a little effort, he pulled and worked on the mass, reshaping it into a beautiful trophy representing a muscular cement mason.

"Your bodies are tough, strong like steel," authoritatively spoke Gerónimo, thumping his own cast-iron chest loudly as he addressed the group.

"We have trained you well and you are the equal of any man in strength and fortitude. Pelón, let me see your muscle."

Pelón flexed a bicep, holding his rock-hard arm in a taut pose that made his fist tremble from the rigidity of the steel-belted muscles. It was a scale model of Hercules, seemingly cast from a mold patterned after the classic statues of history.

The bronze replica of Atlas felt like crumbling plaster as Gerónimo wrapped a claw-like hand around the bumpy bicep, squeezing the rock-hard muscle into sponge. It was to Pelón's credit that he showed no pain, enduring the maestro's vise-grip with the resolute face of an Indian.

"Gerónimo was kind to you," whispered Santos as Gerónimo proceeded along the apprentices on his tour of inspection. "He only *felt* your muscle. If he had really *squeezed* . . . . ."

Pelón was too involved in fighting the urge to faint to let his imagination tell him of the maestro's potential. He could hear the maestro's grunts of approval as he examined the other apprentices.

"You guys have about fifteen minutes to get ready. You will be held by your ankles while you trowel with both hands. Make sure your trowels have no nicks in them and make sure you greñudos fix that long hair so it doesn't get in the way while you work. One of you will get to rest while the other five trowel. You have all studied the ways of the machine. All you have to do is copy it. It is simple," stated Gerónimo matter of factly.

"No wonder they call that thing an upside-down helicopter. Bambi, I don't think it would be a good idea for us to try and trowel like the machines. They have a centered drive device that allows them to go in a circle. We're liable to tie ourselves in knots if we try to imitate them."

Bambi was tying the final bow on the ribbon holding Pelón's braid. They were standing in front of Capitán Jaf Ipaf's truck, Pelón looking over the machines while Bambi arranged his braids, lacing pink ribbon through Pelón's hair.

"There, all you have to do is put your bandana on and you're ready Pelón," said Bambi, admiring the handiwork he'd done on Pelón's hair.

"Santos," called Pelón as the maestro walked by. "Are we really going to compete against each other in this event? How are we going to be judged?"

"We want to see how fast you can work and how much area you can cover, compared to the others. Remember, this is going to be done Chicano style. That means anything goes," offered Santos as he walked towards the large slab.

Minutes later, they were lined up; all but Spanicy who was not in the first heat. The other five leaned over the edge of the slab, their trowels in hand as a maestro stood behind each one, ready to grab their ankles and begin.

"Okay," signalled Gerónimo. "Get on your marks, get set, *go!*"

Tiburón had a slight advantage after a few minutes of activity. As they troweled with mechanical efficiency, they moved in an arc, from their right to their left and back, progressing along the first quarter of the slab's area. Tiburón insured his advantage by reaching out to gouge holes in the area to either side of him. Bambi and Fly'nn Calabera had to work feverishly to patch the holes left by Tiburón.

Fly'nn Calabera quickly made up the distance, thanks to his lank frame and long arms. Bambi was able to pass Tiburón when Fly'nn Calabera executed a perfect delaying tactic. Hesitating as he reached far to his left, Fly'nn Calabera waited for Tiburón to come around. With catlike quickness, the slender Calabera extended a long arm of justice, timing his reach exactly.

Tiburón lost thirty seconds patching up the hole left by his nose when Fly'nn Calabera hooked his arm and knocked him off balance. Bambi and Fly'nn Calabera were neck and neck when Gerónimo signalled for everyone to change partners. Tiburón went to the sidelines as Spanicy was held by Juan Conpala. The diminutive laborer strained under the load while Spanicy toiled with his trowels. Fly'nn Calabera jumped into the lead but lost out to Bambi when he reached too far into Pelón's area in an attempt to dig holes with the point of his trowel. Pelón deftly removed his bandana, slipping it around Fly'nn Calabera's wrist and hooking it to the skinny apprentice's belt buckle.

Spanicy was surprisingly fast, despite the fact that his huge belly was causing some drag. Juan Conpala was too short to hold Spanicy high enough for his stomach to clear the slab. Pelón was closing in on the leader, almost even with Bambi when it was time to change partners again.

Spanicy was able to increase his pace when his new partner, Cubra Vidrios, took over the ankle-holding duties. Cubra was tall enough to ensure Spanicy's stomach had plenty of clearance; thus saving Spanicy the time of having to patch the holes left by his belt buckle. Pelón fought off Tiburón's challenge, coming very close to over-taking Bambi when time was called. Gerónimo announced that the remaining area was too wet to finish. They would have a half-hour rest until the final leg of their competition.

Capitán Jaf Ipaf was sitting on a bank, looking into the distance at the peaks of the far-off range of mountains. Pelón approached quietly, squatting alongside the pensive mason. His usually comical appearance faded as Pelón studied his face. Though Quebra Vidrios was nearly sixty, his face was not wrinkled, except around the eyes, which made him look like he was smiling most of the time. Quebra had once remarked that being a greaser had its advantages. A person with oily skin was less likely to become wrinkled.

Quebra Vidrios' massive shoulders made Pelón's own tired shoulders seem like a shrunken silhouette as their shadows extended over the ground in front of them. Pelón waited patiently, waiting for the *maestro's* indication that he could speak as was the custom.

"Have you ever thought about wild animals, Pelón? Wild animals lead a much harder life. They must constantly exploit their bodies because it is their only means of surviving. But still, they have time to play, moments when they can fool around without having to put everything into the attack and the kill. A hard-working man is somewhat the same."

"What do you mean, maestro?" asked Pelón.

"When you work hard and use your body, then you can play and rest with a true appreciation for what God gave you. The playing and the rest, they serve to regenerate your spirit so you can go back to work feeling better, stronger. It is a fine line, though. Too much play or rest can make you lazy when it comes to work. Too much work can make it impossible for you to summon the energy to play and you never seem to get enough rest."

"You see those mountains over there, Pelón? What do they say to you? Can you hear what they are saying?"

Pelón stared at the mountains, remembering and thinking; reflecting on life. He did not know how to answer Quebra Vidrios. Quietly, he offered the maestro his thoughts.

"They say everything has a beginning and an end. All that lies in between has within it what is on both ends of the process. Life and death are one, part of something else we can know nothing about until we are removed from that process."

"Yes," sighed Quebra Vidrios, looking reflectively at the distant mountains. "We are part of something that is truly awesome and marvelous. Yet it is nothing because even the most permanent of things will crumble to dust and the dust will float off to dissolve in the air. Pelón, what did you learn in school or in all the books you read that could possibly explain such a strange thing as life? I am not such a smart man. All I know is what I have learned by watching the world around me. I see God outside of this whole thing, but yet I know He is in every little bit of everything. What are the secrets of all the maestros combined compared to such a mystery? What can possibly explain that mysterious and wonderful process?"

"Maybe something called the Dialectical Process can explain some of it, maestro," offered Pelón to the now quiet Quebra. Pelón had never seen Quebra in such a mood. He was usually less gruff than Gerónimo, but still more physical and less philosophical than Santos. Quebra liked to joke a lot, but he also possessed a temper which quickly cooled any apprentice who made an error or stepped out of line during the instruction.

"In this process that we can call life, there is a starting point or thesis. This thesis is met by its opposite which is a contradiction. This opposite is called the antithesis. These two things, the thesis and the antithesis, combine through a struggle of the counteracting forces to create a synthesis. The synthesis then becomes the starting point for another chain of events and you have another contradicting antithesis meeting with this synthesis. But remember, maestro, the synthesis is a new starting point, so it is no longer the synthesis. It is a new thesis. The struggle between the new thesis and its contradictory antithesis leads to another synthesis and so on."

"What happens? How does the change take place?" inquired Quebra thoughtfully, his eyes telling of the attempt to understand Pelón's explanation. He was listening carefully, noting Pelón's words attentively.

"Well, the two contradictions, the thesis and the antithesis, struggle against each other and then there is a sudden and spontaneous action called praxis which takes place. That is how the synthesis occurs, maestro."

"That is very interesting, Pelón. Did you learn that in a book?" asked Quebra, repeating the new words to himself so as not to forget them.

Gerónimo's yell to return to the troweling interrupted their session. Moments later, Pelón was perspiring heavily in the

warm sun, troweling madly in an effort to keep up with Fly'nn
Calabera who had taken the lead. Bambi stood aside as the competition continued. The raspy scraping of their trowels resounded in the air as the maestros held their ankles firmly. Capitán Jaf Ipaf cleared his throat loudly and began to speak,
hoping he would correctly remember what Pelón had explained
to him moments earlier.

"Oye, Santos. Do you still read a lot of books?"

"When I have time. It is a good thing, a man can learn much
from books. Did you ever read the book I lent you three years
ago?" inquired Santos, recalling that Capitán Jaf Ipaf had only
reluctantly agreed to take the book home when it was offered.
He did not like to read much.

"Oh no, I am always so busy and I started reading some
other books. I read a very good book. It told all about how we
can figure out the world. I can't remember the name of it right
now, but it was very hard to read; with a lot of big words in it,"
explained Capitán Jaf Ipaf.

"I think it must be for people going to college and for
teachers because I had a very hard time understanding the big
words. But I think I have it pretty well in mind now. I was saving it for our next mitote, but I think I shall tell you about it
while it is fresh in my mind," spoke Capitán Jaf Ipaf as though
he were about to deliver a lecture without the use of notes.
Even his tone of voice changed as he began his professorial delivery.

"Oye, compadre. You be sure to listen because some of the
words are pretty hard to understand. Okay?"

"Oh churro, compadre, I will hear good," answered Juan
Conpala. The other maestros kept an attentive ear pointed at
Capitán Jaf Ipaf as they monitored the performance of the ap-
prentices.

"Life is like a big chain but we never have explained how
the links were put together and how the first link was started.
We don't even know if the chain goes on and on, or if it is just a
big circle and there really is no master link or what. It could go

on and on, in a line, or circle back and join the starting point.
¿Verdad?"

The maestros voiced their agreement and Capitán Jaf Ipaf
continued.

"Pues anyway, you start off with a link, any link. This is
called the . . . . ."

Capitán Jaf Ipaf hesitated as he tried to recall the word
Pelón had used.

"It is called the Ceaseless," spoke Capitán Jaf Ipaf with authority.

"And then you have something that is the opposite putting
pressure on the Ceaseless. It is called the . . . . . it is called the
Ants Tea Seat. That is because many years ago, the ormigas
ruled the world and the King and Queen used to like to sit
around and drink tea when they talked about important stuff.
Are you with me so far, compadre?"

"Como no, compadre," replied Juan Conpala. "Estoy yendo
al night eschool for to learn Ingleesh."

"Muy bien," said Capitán Jaf Ipaf, continuing the talk.

"The Ceaseless and the other one have a fight and you get
something else. It is called the Sensibleness because a long time
ago a maestro showed the gavachos how to explain the mysteries of the world. He told them, sencillo no es, and they wrote
many books about this great man's ideas."

Santos, quick to digest Capitán Jaf Ipaf's words, asked a
question.

"Quebra, what happens when there is a fight between these
things. Is it like when two worlds collide and there is an explo-
sion?"

"Yes, but it is also so small that there is hardly a sound because this happens in everything, large and small. A very magical
thing takes place and it is called Pr . . . Pr . . . Pra. No, no, it is
called Pick-up Sticks. You see, every time this thing happens,
everything falls down like a house made of sticks. So then God
reaches down and picks up the sticks and builds a new house.
So it is called Pick-Up Sticks."

The maestros were very interested in Capitán Jaf Ipaf's explanation of the mysteries of the world and had much to offer in the way of observations as the competition continued. It was still early afternoon when the work was completed and the apprentices awaited the results of the day's test.

The group climbed to the top of a hill overlooking the building project. The other side of the hill, a sheer drop of some one hundred feet, offered them a view of the ground below as the nervous apprentices peered over the edge of the cliff. They had each been instructed to carry a ten foot length of two-by-twelve lumber up the hill.

Gerónimo rolled a large boulder near the spot on which the curious initiates stood. Extending a board over the cliff, Santos held it while Gerónimo placed the boulder atop the end touching the hard ground. Each of the maestros then took the remaining five boards and extended them over the cliff, standing on the grounded end. Six makeshift diving boards poked out from the cliff-top, the apprentices looking at each other with puzzled faces.

"Spanicy, you are heavier than any of us. You take the board with the boulder. Go on, walk to the edge," ordered Gerónimo.

Spanicy's heart was not the only one ceasing its beat as the apprentices felt their stomachs drop. Only Gerónimo's unbelievably fierce glare forced Spanicy to walk the plank. He stood shivering, the board bowing slightly as Spanicy closed his eyes after a quick peek downward.

One by one, the apprentices were ordered to the edge of the boards. None dared more than a fleeting glance at the bottom. Pelón looked at his fellow apprentices, his own fear mirrored in their faces. He closed his eyes and began praying. Gerónimo's deep voice came from behind the group of trembling neophytes.

"Only one of you will go on to the next step. Only one will have the chance to fly to new heights and soar with the spirits of the world. The rest of you will have to wait for another time. The trophy I made is but a paltry offering compared to the gift one shall shortly receive."

"You are all fortunate. But one is more fortunate than the rest, so stop sniveling and shaking!" thundered Gerónimo, the vibrations from his voice causing the planks to begin flapping like tuning forks. "Are there any questions before we announce who predominated in the test today?"

Pelón's halting voice was carried by the brisk breeze as he asked the question that had been puzzling him and the other apprentices. Because they were taught only to speak when spoken to, they had shared their bewilderment with each other. Pelón decided it was time to ask.

"Maestro. Where is Jr.? Why wasn't he here today?"

"That will soon be answered. Are the maestros ready?"

Cubra, standing behind Bambi and holding the two-by-twelve in place with his weight, nodded. Juan Conpala, holding a forty-pound rock in his hands to compensate for his lack of weight, stood behind Fly'nn Calabera, nodding his readiness. Santos stood behind Tiburón. Escoba kept Cockroach from tilting the balance. That left Gerónimo on Pelón's plank and the boulder holding Spanicy's board.

"Keep a stout heart and have your will always at the ready. Others have gone before you and others will follow. Only those with strong hearts and spirits are chosen. Before we announce the winner, Santos will present the proper chant to commemorate this solemn occasion."

Santos was clearing his throat, about to step forward for his role in the ceremony. He quickly changed his mind, deciding to address the group from his position, lest the center of balance be broached and Tiburón launched prematurely.

> Mi mi mi, la la la,
> momento de silencio, ningún ha ha.
> Dáme chancita de preparar la voz,
> hay que pensar que decir a os.
> Como dije ahem y salió el pollo,
> si caen al suelo dejarán un oyo.
> Allá abajo no hay trampolina,
> tampoco encontrarán una piscina.

Cual será quien sale con diploma,
irán como piedra o una paloma.
No se pongan pánicos muchachos de Aztlán,
Al cabo de los séis solo ganará juan.

"One of you will go into the next phase of instruction," stated Gerónimo at the completion of the chant. "It is a much more difficult part with many responsibilities. Today's winner is now an official . . . . . Drop-out!" said Gerónimo as he stepped back to release the winner.

PELON DROPS OUT

CHAPTER NUEVE

PELON DROPS OUT

Pelón hung in midair for what seemed an eternity. His mind
was still racing madly, filled with a thousand thoughts, all pos-
sessing a timeless clarity and individuality that made time come
to a halt as he stood suspended in the atmosphere. He was not
sure if he should look down or to the sky for his heart. It had
jumped from his body when Gerónimo's announcement came,
leaving his body in a dramatic leap. His heart's direction could
not be ascertained by the momentarily dazed Pelón. He wasn't
sure if it had flown upward through his mouth or downward
through his afterburner.

What was happening? Was he expected to assume the body
of a bird and fly? Would he find some heretofore unknown
power that would allow him to turn into some other form
which would defy gravity? His mind was a mad mixture of ideas
as he envisioned himself crashing to the earth, the victim of
some cruel test of powers he did not know about.

He was not prepared for such a feat. He had only heard the
maestros mention the ability of men with power to perform
belief-defying acts as changing into an animal. He experienced a
momentary feeling of dislike for the maestros. It was not right
for them to do such a thing when they had not prepared him
for this moment. He would surely be killed in the fall. Would
the price of graduation be his life? Is that what being a Drop-
out meant?

He looked back towards the group, his face mirroring his
fear and shock as the maestros smiled reassuringly, waving like
fathers viewing their new-born child through the maternity
ward window. Pelón felt like Wile Y. Coyote who has just
realized he has once again been victimized by the elusive Road-
runner. Summoning every bit of courage, Pelón closed his eyes
and prepared to accept the outcome.

Flapping his arms wildly, he noticed a curious thing occur-
ring. The timelessness he had experienced as he dangled with
nothing but the waiting ground far below disappeared. Time
seemed to accelerate, matching the pace of his frantic beating at
the air with his outstretched arms. His body began moving at

the rate of thirty-two feet per second and his arms were moving at the rate of forty-six flaps per second, but tiring fast. His rapidly fatiguing arms were barely able to compensate for the pull of gravity upon his mass when he heard his name called.

It was Jr. Looking up with a start, Pelón saw Jr. floating towards him, reaching out with life preserving hands for his friend. Two eagles supported Jr. on his rescuing flight. They were painted on the wings of Jr.'s new Hang-Glider.

Pelón reached desperately for Jr., feeling his newly found heart leave again as his grasp slipped and he resumed falling. He was fortunate that only that morning, Jr. had tied a long tail to his Hang-Glider, wanting to test its effects on the newly purchased device. Jr. executed a stall, bringing the tail within reach of Pelón's flailing hands. Pelón was saved by a chain of limpiadores. The pieces of flour sacks used as cloth napkins were Pelón's salvation. They were very handy around the house because they were large enough that a large family could use them without wiping on the same spot someone else had put his mouth to.

Pelón's weight made handling a little difficult, but Jr. managed to descend without mishap. Jr. was happily folding his new toy when the group of maestros and apprentices came down the hill to stand around the still quivering Pelón.

"Why didn't you turn into a Hawk or a Hummingbird even?" grunted Gerónimo while Pelón massaged the area where his heart was thumping against his heaving chest.

"Santos, you had better show Pelón how to survive such events. Maybe we should give him some chilepuro extra extra so he can take off like a balloon when you let go of the untied end," stated Gerónimo seriously, his finger imitating the erratic flight of a released child's balloon. Pelón was shocked to see that Gerónimo was finger-painting in the air, a stream of colors pouring from his fingertip like Sparklers on a dark Fourth of July night.

The maestro changed the pattern of his drawing, writing words with his finger that appeared in the afternoon sun like

Pelón hung in midair for what seemed an eternity.

multicolored neon. Pelón concentrated as he read the sentences which said:

"Anybody can fly high when they take chilepuro or magic mocos. Even a lead balloon will float when filled with the smoke from verdolagas, ojas de elote and tolondrones palos preguntones. But only those with heart and will can soar on a Natural High."

The apprentices chatted with the newly arrived Jr., admiring his new Hang-Glider. Fly'nn Calabera and Spanicy, accompanied by Tiburón and Cockroach, eagerly offered to drive Jr. back to the ridge from which he had launched his new flying device. The maestros huddled in a group while Bambi and Pelón picked up the tools. Santos told Pelón to wait for him at the top of the hill from which he had been graduated into his next phase of apprenticeship. Bambi was excused and everyone left the jobsite but Santos.

Pelón waited for the maestro to join him, watching the picture-postcard sunset as Santos walked up the hill. The sun was hidden behind a horizontal column of clouds, their form looking as though they had been molded by a child playing with cotton-candy. Brilliant orange hues charged the sunset with breath-taking stillness, the surroundings seeming to come alive with an eerie glow from the last splash of light from the sun.

"It is the most thrilling of times," came Santos' soft voice as he sat next to Pelón. "A sunrise is exciting, filling you with a sense of majesty and power. But a sunset such as we are witnessing almost brings you to the point where you are one with the mysteries of the world. The power of the sun releases its hold on the earth and a stillness comes over everything. You can almost feel your heart reaching out to join the horizon, wanting to stand at the juncture so you can forever be at peace with the world. It is as though the earth's sigh of welcome to the night is pulling you toward the mouth of time as the world takes in a deep breath, the wind almost taking your hand and leading you toward that point where light and darkness merge."

"It is not the same feeling you felt when Gerónimo let go of the board, is it, Pelón?" chuckled Santos, his eyes twinkling with delight.

"I did not know what to think maestro. I thought perhaps I might become a bird or that you maestros might show me some new power that would allow me to walk on air. It is said that brujos have such powers and can do anything. Can a man acquire the powers that I have heard about, or is it in the imagination?"

"It is everywhere, all around you," said Santos dramatically, waving his hand in all directions. "It is here," he continued, placing his finger to his forehead to indicate his mind. "It is here," he said, touching his chest to mean his heart.

"Pelón, where did you get the idea that we are brujos? We do not believe in witchcraft or evil spells. Did you come to us because you thought we are brujos?"

"Yes, maestro, I used to hear the whispers of the people saying that Gerónimo and you, and the rest of the cementeros, were brujos. And the day I first went to Gerónimo's house, his wife was very angry about something, yelling at Gerónimo and calling him viejo brujo."

"Ay muchacho," sighed Santos. "Perhaps the candles they used to put in your ears when you were an altar boy left a little wax and you did not hear properly. She meant viejo bruto. People are always saying we are brutos because we work so hard."

"But where do your powers come from, maestro, if not from witchcraft. Where did you learn those recipes and the chants?"

"That will be divulged later. But for now, you can keep it in mind that you are among brutos, not brujos. Would you like to go with those three Indians you met that day at my house? Would you like to talk once again with your Papá Ricardo? Whatever you want, it is within your power to accomplish, within certain limits. You have already gained the necessary power for such feats of heart."

"What are the limitations, Santos?"

"They are the limitations placed upon you by your place in

the world. Everything about you combines to give you power and to limit that power in such a way that will lead to a proper result. Your heart is the true test of your ability, my son. It may not seem fair, but a good heart sometimes places you at a disadvantage compared to people who do not limit their actions according to their heart. They may threaten you if your paths should cross, but you would survive."

"If it were not for your caring about others, you might never need to concern yourself with people who have powers that are not tempered by heart. You could control your world to such an extent that you would never be bothered by the acts of others. But as it is, you choose to care and it shall be the thing that both limits and frees you until the day you die."

"Responsibility slowly grows as you do, becoming a way of acting as you mature. As your power and will increase, so does the responsibility and awareness of your place in the world. You become a man, realizing you cannot have things as you would want them because your wishes are clouded by selfishness. The selfishness would not actually temper your actions, unless you felt responsibility. But since you do, you find yourself in a position where you have to make profound decisions about your actions."

"That is why there are those whose powers are greater than yours who can threaten you. They do not have the responsibility to temper their selfishness and they make full use of their available power for their ends. You have a choice. You can become as they are or walk your own path and place your destiny in God's hands and try to acquire faith to sustain you as you walk the path of life. The second way is much harder than you can imagine because there may never be a time when you know if you are walking in the right direction. It is something you must live with until your last second on earth, my son. Even as death comes for you, your eyes will be blind to the landmarks that only your heart can follow."

"Would you like to embark on a little adventure, Pelón? I can give you passage to the land of those Indians you met if you wish."

"Will I be gone long? I would like to go, but it is getting late," said Pelón, his eagerness for adventure barely contained as Santos' reminder about responsibility echoed in his mind.

"No, it won't take long. You will be back in a short time as far as this world goes. Close your eyes and I will send you there. When you have learned to chant, you will be able to go without my help. But for now, I must send you there with my words."

Pelón felt the cool breeze billowing around him as Santos began a chant. The maestro was apparently banging two rocks together as he began humming. Their clicking sound stopped as Santos quietly spoke the words that would send Pelón to the Ain't-Syet-Land of the Warrior's Spirit.

> Pelón, Pelón, Cabeza de Melón,
> sana sana, colita de rana.
> Cierre los ojos mi cabezón,
> irás en un viaje a otra mañana.
> Eres tan tonto que querías volar,
> hasta los pájaros se rieron a wachar.
> Te dejamos colgado a ver que pasará,
> buscando algo que te salvará.
> Que no hubiera llegado el mentado,
> te caerías como pato desplumado.
>
> Ahora estas listo, ojalá y te conserva,
> recuerde que no debes fumar ningúna yerba.
> Si quieres ser hombre nunca te piques,
> si buscas que mascar, compre unos chícles.
> Eso de ser malcriado no vale,
> si te ofrecen tentación, diles chale.
>
> Yo no digo que no puedes gozar,
> si tienes sed, tomate el mar.
> Quien soy yo que te dijiera no lo hagas,
> el que tiene hambre hasta se come verdolagas.
> Eres igual que un chamaquito,
> todo a la boca con buen apetito.

La curiosidad ha matado a muchos gatos,
lo mismo se dice de los vatos.
Ahora si quieres escapar la prisión,
ponte a usar la imaginación.

Pelón, Pelón, Cabeza de Melón,
te dicen al revés y tienen razón.
A poco te cres que estas bien y sano,
portandote así como un loco Chicano.
Como me dijiste aquella vez?
Soy combinación del número tres.
Europeo con Indio resultó en tu gente,
pero mucha televisión atrasó la mente.

Santos' voice faded as a rumbling noise like distant thunder began intensifying. The thunder seemed to grow louder, as if a huge boulder were rolling down a hill, causing more rocks to dislodge. The avalanching ceased abruptly with a loud cracking noise that startled Pelón. He opened his eyes quickly, finding the brightness hard to manage. His eyes had grown accustomed to the dim light of the sunset and were shielded from all light during Santos' chanting. It took a few seconds for Pelón's vision to clear.

He found himself seated on a ledge overlooking a clear stream. He could see the rocks lining the bottom of the stream, the water flowing in a lapping rhythm along the narrow stretch of the creek-bed. A lone willow tree drooped lazily some twenty yards away. A lizard streaked momentarily across a nearby boulder, its tail flicking a goodbye as it seemed to be sucked into the narrow crevice between two rocks.

Various types of cactus dotted the rust-brown landscape, the beauty of the area enhanced by patches of colorful ground-cover. Even the rocks had an organic quality to them, an alluring attractiveness that filled Pelón with contentment. The scene was the epitome of tranquility, each thing catching the eye, resting naturally in the setting in such a way that combined to bring peace to Pelón.

A movement above, in the rocks to Pelón's left, caught his attention. The upper body of one of the Indians was visible as Pelón looked up. The Indian disappeared, popping up behind a large rock halfway down the hill. He was now clearly visible, making his way down at a brisk pace, jumping from rock to rock as he descended towards Pelón. The scar on his face became discernible as he approached Pelón. Pelón was standing, waiting for the Indian.

"Have you decided what it is you want of this world?" asked the Indian after a long silence in which they stared at each other. There was something about the Indian's stare that made Pelón unable to shift his gaze from his dark peering eyes. He had wanted to examine the Indian, to note the details of his face and body as a matter of curiosity. Instead, he found himself captivated by the Indian's eyes, his mind becoming a blank until the Indian spoke.

"I want to be a warrior and to know all the secrets of a warrior," blurted Pelón to his own surprise. "I want to smoke things and eat herbs that give me visions and power. I want to be invincible; stronger than any man so that nothing can hurt me. I want to be fearless and have happiness."

"Would you be willing to give up the other world for these things? What if I told you the things you ask for are impossible to grant. What if I told you that only in your dreams can you have the things you ask for. What if I told you this is a dream?" spoke the Indian.

"But this is not a dream. I know it is real," protested Pelón.

"Sit down, we must talk," said the Indian, leaning back to rest on a sandstone ledge. His stare shifted from Pelón's eyes, looking into the sky. His eyes changed remarkably, losing their cold fierceness, turning soft as he faced the horizon. Pelón felt as though the Indian might even cry, the eyes glistening with moisture that told of deeply touching emotion.

"You have a child's heart Chopopóte. It is for that reason that you do not see me as I really am. The same holds true for everything you see around you right now. Yes, this place is real; I am real. But your imagination is standing between you and the real appearance of this world. Whether you know it or not, your heart prompts your imagination to take hold of what you are witnessing so that everything can appear in a way that will not harm you."

"Do you remember the time you were captured by Santos' eyes and went to the land of your brothers who first called you by that name, Chopopóte? You turned down an offer from the eagle to ride your brother, the stallion."

"Oh yes, that was the first time I had ever heard that name and talked to animals. It was a great experience," gushed Pelón, happily recalling the incident.

"Well, what if I told you that you could only have such an experience again if you forfeited the right to ever visit with me or your grandfather. What if you had to make such a choice. Would you give up the chance to talk to my friends in exchange for the world of talking animals?"

"I do not know," replied Pelón. "Why would I have to make such a choice? Can't I have all those things? Do you mean there are no talking animals in this place?" asked Pelón, looking around for any sign of a creature. A lone bird flew by, too far away for Pelón to tell what kind of bird it was.

"How can you be a warrior if there is nothing to struggle against?" was the Indian's next question for the apprentice. "I know what it is you want, what you seek, but I want you to say it. You will better learn a lesson if it comes from your own mouth."

Pelón thought for a while but could not figure out what the Indian was talking about.

"Maybe these aren't worlds at all, Pelón. Perhaps they are in your imagination after all. Does that make sense to you? Can you understand that all of this may be real but yet imaginary?"

"Yes, I think so. But I still don't know what it is that I want, not the way you have confused me. I told you, I want to know what a warrior knows and to have power. I want to be invincible and happy. Right now, I want to be clear-headed, so why don't you tell me what it is you think I really want," stated Pelón with frustration.

"I will tell you. Maybe you will learn something, I don't know. You are certainly not very good at patiently extracting the secrets of the world. What you want is to match your moods. You either wish to have power to control the world in such a way that makes life easy for you, or you want to be able to go into other worlds that satisfy the mood you are feeling."

"If you are sad, you want a world that responds to your sadness. If you feel adventuresome, you want the world to offer you thrills and adventure. If you feel like thinking seriously, you want to listen to someone speak profound thoughts to you. When you feel small and helpless, you want to have power to make yourself feel big and in control of the world. It is very simple. You want to be a child."

"No I don't. I want to be a man, a man of knowledge and power," stated Pelón firmly. "I am not a child and I don't want to be a child. I want to be a man."

"Okay, what if that means you will have to walk around that hill over there and fight it out with the cu-cui," said the Indian seriously, pointing to a nearby hill.

"All you have to do is close your eyes for a few seconds. e yourself time to make up your mind. When you open your eyes, your heart will have made the decision for you. You will either be ready to walk to the other side of that hill and meet with the cu-cui, or you will wake up and be in the everyday world again. Now close your eyes and we will see what happens."

Pelón closed his eyes and the rumbling noise began. A loud snap once again opened his eyes with a start. It was dark and Santos was sitting quietly next to him.

"Well, how was it, Pelón? Did you see the three Indians?"

"I only saw one of them, maestro. But I couldn't understand what he was saying so I came back," said Pelón, hoping Santos would believe his white lie. "I guess I am not ready. He was saying things that were too complicated for me."

Pelón hoped the darkness would hide his deception and perhaps Santos would not be able to detect he was fibbing. Pelón hoped the maestro would not ask any more questions.

"Think about what he said, Pelón. It is late and we had better go now. It has been a hard day and you will sleep well after today's experiences," said Santos as they made their way down the hill toward their vehicles.

PELON DROPS OUT

CHAPTER DIEZ

PELON DROPS OUT

"Pelón, you're very quiet. Is something wrong, are you worried about something?" asked Mrs. Palomares as the family was seated at the supper table. She noticed that her son did not so much as offer a weak protest when his brother Bartolo grabbed four tortillas from the stack she had just placed on the table. Mr. Palomares was too busy reading the Lombligo Lantern to notice that Bartolo had greedily snatched the tortillas, sitting on three of them in order to have a sufficient stock-pile until his mother could make more.

Mrs. Palomares scolded Bartolo, making him put the tortillas back in the wicker basket where she had placed the fresh stack, wrapped in a limpiador to keep them warm. She returned to the kitchen after reprimanding her husband for reading at the table. As she made more tortillas, she wondered about Pelón, his quiet mood warning that something was amiss. He was usually active, even at the table, sharing what he had learned that day about construction work.

Pelón's parents had not protested much when Pelón quit school to work for Gerónimo Vidrios. They did not know much about the educational system, having both dropped out before reaching high school. They had been happy to have such a precocious child, proud that the teachers called them in from time to time to explain they were giving their son more tests or advancing him yet another grade. He was but fourteen when he entered college, winning a scholarship to a nearby private school called Behavioral Research Accelerated Institute for Neat-wits. They were glad that B.R.A.I.N. was close enough for Pelón to take the bus.

The Palomares, after a long discussion, had agreed to let their son enroll in the school, with the stipulation that he would spend three hours each afternoon doing chores and playing. They did not want Pelón to become overly involved in his studies and miss out on a normal adolescence. So it was that they were not very disappointed when Pelón, on his eighteenth birthday, advised them that he was leaving school in order to learn a trade. It would be a good rest for him and he could always return to his studies.

His genius and long hours of study had kept him from having a life like his friends. The Palomares understood that Pelón needed some time away from school. Though he might be advanced intellectually, they knew their son was somewhat retarded in other respects. Working would give him the opportunity to learn about normal life. It would better prepare him to deal with the world if he were to meet other people and lead a somewhat more average existence for a while.

"Mom, I'm going for a walk. I'll be back in a while, okay?"

Mrs. Palomares turned to Pelón who had brought his plate to the kitchen. He placed it on the counter, the silverware and glass stacked neatly on the plate. She appreciated his helpfulness and smiled.

"Don't stay out too late, mi'jo. Don't talk to the pachucos and watch out for the cu-cui. Que Dios te bendiga," she said, hoping her blessing would keep her son from harm as he walked out the back door into the night.

He walked along the sidewalk in front of his house until he came to La Oya Road. Turning right, he waited for a car to pass before crossing the street. He was alone with his thoughts as he approached Enano Crecido's store. Pelón was thinking about the small lie he had told Santos, feeling guilt at knowing he had deceived the maestro and withheld information regarding his encounter with the Indian. He was also disappointed in himself, remembering that he had been afraid of meeting the cu-cui. He did not want to go to bed in such an unsettled state, fearing what might happen during his sleep.

A group of guys stood around the phone booth at one corner of the store. One of them was using the pay phone, laughing and talking while two other guys added comments and suggested topics of conversation. Three others leaned against the store's stucco wall, watching the cars that would pass now and then.

They were Pelón's age, a couple of them a little older. He remembered them from grammar school. He had left them behind when he skipped the eighth grade at the age of eleven. Once Pelón left La Oya Elementary, his progress was even more

accelerated. The small school in the colonia had not begun test-
ing him until the third grade.

"Orale, cuñado, what are you doing, ese?" said the tallest of
the group. His name was Elistanasio but they called him Mangas. Pelón could not recall ever having seen him wearing anything but a long-sleeve shirt, even in P.E.

Pelón smiled a greeting, turning his attention to the store
window where he could see Mr. Crecido bargaining with a customer. A car passed, rapping its pipes; the loud mufflers a greeting which the group acknowledged. Pelón turned to see a white
primered Chevelle bounce down La Oya Road, barely inches
from the ground. A fancy-scroll lettering on the side read, "Sí
Sí Rider."

"Hey, Pelón, com 'ere, ese," beckoned one of the guys. It
was Rolosejiado, whom everyone called Rollo. Spider and
Stimey turned from the phone booth to stand alongside Rollo,
Mangas and Tatoo. Guidi-guidi stayed on the phone, obviously
talking to a girl.

"Where you been, Pelón? Whuf's hapnin?" asked Tatoo.

"How's your sister, Pelón? Tell her I said hi," stated Mangas.

"You still going to college, man? What kinda stuff you
learning?" inquired Rollo.

"I was taking Quadraflex Terrestrial Theory and Binary
Bilbous Bracketing," offered Pelón. "But I dropped out. I quit
school and I'm learning to be a cement mason," he said proudly.

"That's casual," said Tatoo. "I'm looking for a job. Know
where I can get one, ese?"

"No. Why don't you go to the Unemployment or ask Mantecoso Mastrucha at the second store."

La Oya had three stores; known as the first, the second and
the third, according to their order along the main street. If
someone from the East side of La Oya ran into a person from
the West end, they would have to refer to the stores by name.
The first store to someone from the East side was the third to

someone from the opposite end of the colonia and vice versa. So there was Enano Crecido's store, Mantecoso Mastrucha's and the Carneusada Brother's Market.

"Chale with that jale," stated Tatoo, voicing his disapproval of the jobs Mantecoso Mastrucha contracted for local people. "Puro carwash and strawberry picking, that's all that dude lines up for people."

"Hey Pelón, you want to go for a cruise with us? Fluffy is coming to pick us up in a while. Hang around and you can go for a little ride with us," offered Rollo, remembering that Leroy MacGreengold, the only gavacho pachuco around was on his way to pick them up. Fluffy was an honorary Chicano. He dressed and talked like the rest of the guys and he could speak Spanish and street-talk as well as anyone.

During the 1940's, the Pachuco was exemplified by the Zoot Zooters who wore Zoot Suits. The more casual attire of pachucos usually consisted of a Pendleton shirt, black pants or khakis. Pelón, remembering his mother's cautioning voice, decided to decline their offer to take him for a ride. Though he wanted to see for himself why his mother did not want him associating with them, he decided not to go against her instructions.

"No thanks," said Pelón. "I have to be home early."

"Hijo, what a tapado," sighed Tatoo. "Come on, ese, we'll get you home by curfew. You can even ride next to a window instead of the middle. Just be sure your sobaco doesn't peel the paint off the door, man."

Tatoo was referring to the classic cruising position in which the guys sat low in the seat with an arm hanging out as they cruised the streets. The most famous of the local lowriders was a guy called Mocho. He received his nickname because he showed true class and style one day when a group of guys decided to cruise to the mountains to see the snow. The prime example of toughness, Mocho steadfastly refused to raise the window, braving frost-bite and scorning the offer of a glove and jacket as he cruised clad in a t-shirt in his proud pose as a bad lowrider.

"You still going to college, man? What kind of stuff you learning?"

"I was taking Quadraflex Terrestrial Theory and Binary Bilbous Bracketing. But I dropped out. I quit school and I'm learning to be a cement mason," he said proudly.

"That's casual," said Tatoo.

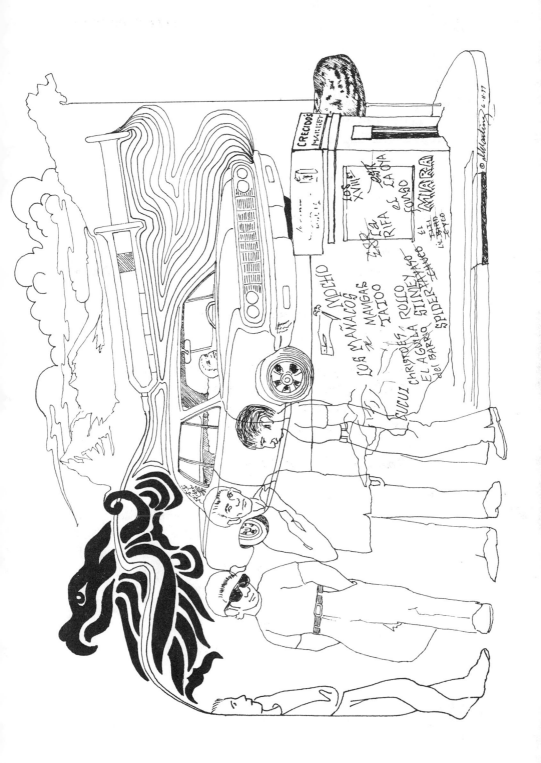

On warm summer nights, Mocho could now be seen cruising with the guys, his head barely visible over the seat, his left arm draped over the side of the car. He liked to cruise shirtless on warm nights, his arm bearing a tatoo which read, Todo se paga. On cold winter nights, Mocho rode on the right side of the car, his window open in defiance of the weather, the empty long-sleeve Pendleton hanging over the door.

The doctors who removed Mocho's frozen arm after the history-making cruise said his stubborn attitude cost him a limb. They did not know it had won him a place in the annals of famous lowriders. His nickname was retired, painted on the highest spot on the wall of Enano Crecido's store. A banner depicting a shirt-sleeve waving in the breeze decorated Mocho's spot on the Loco Lowrider's Wall of Fame.

"Pelón, how about donating some coin to our defense committee," coaxed Rollo. "Our club, The Magnificent Mañacos, started a legal defense fund and we need some money 'cause our Homeboys are always getting busted on humbugs. The other day, the Placa popped Stimey for shooting up in the bathroom at the Boy's Club."

"You mean he was firing a gun in the restroom?" inquired the astounded Pelón. He certainly would not contribute to such an unworthy cause as defending a lawbreaker.

"Nah, man, he's a diabetic and they rousted him on some humbug law about using a hyperdermic in public," explained Spider.

"Yeah, they even took away the kit he was using and it belongs to me. I loaned him my kit and those dirty Placa complicated it for evidence," came Guidi-guidi's angry remark.

"What's a kit?" asked the ignorant Pelón, overlooking Guidi-guidi's grammatical error.

"One a these things," stated Spider, pulling a small box from his back pocket. Opening the box, he displayed the contents to the curious Pelón who peered with interest at the goods.

"What's the spoon and the rubber band for?" asked Pelón.

"Hijo, don't you know nothing?" sighed Tatoo with disgust. "The rubber band is for when you get a shot and you want the vein to pop out so you can put the medicine in the right place. The spoon is in case we run into any epileptics. We like to help people out, you know. Sometimes you can keep one of those people from swallowing their tongue with a spoon. But the cops won't leave us alone, man. They think we use the needle for something else. You know we wouldn't do those things, Pelón," smiled Tatoo innocently.

Pelón had heard that the pachucos sometimes put nasty things in their veins. He was glad he had gone against his mother's advice and talked to the guys. He might never have seen their side of the story and grown up believing the stories about the pachucos.

"Yeah, Pelón, you oughta go back to school and be a lawyer so you can come back to the barrios and stand up for us," stated Rollo. "Them judges and the Placa keep putting us down, man. We are being updressed by the system."

"You mean oppressed?" asked Pelón helpfully.

"That's what I said, chump, they keep pressing. They won't slack off my case. The other day they hassled me and said I was trying to break into a house. They said I was going to steal stuff so I could buy junk. See how bad they are, Pelón? They wouldn't believe me when I told them I was looking for a friend of mine and I had the wrong house. I was only sticking my head through the window 'cause I thought he was asleep and couldn't hear me knocking. It was a mistake man, anybody can get the wrong address. And why would I want to steal junk to buy more junk? Tell me that, Pelón."

Pelón was considering Rollo's case. Perhaps he had better come out more often and get to know the guys better. Maybe they were misunderstood and victimized by other people's ignorance. He would have to ask Santos. His mother would be too protective and let gossip and popular beliefs affect her judgment. It would be best to consult with Santos on this matter.

"Hey, so let us have five bucks for a worthy cause, Pelón," suggested Spider.

"I only have four dollars. You guys can have three but I have to keep one for gas."

Pelón was barely able to hear what Spider whispered to Stimey as he handed Rollo the three dollars.

"Tres bolas? Wow, we can't even score a nickel's worth of reds with that."

Rollo, noting that Pelón overheard, offered Pelón an explanation.

"He means that since the club only keeps one per cent of what we collect, we still need two more dollars so we can take out two cents and have a nickel to buy some pistachios out of the machine in the store."

"Oh, well, I can fix that," said Pelón happily. Reaching into his pocket, he pulled out some more money. Handing Spider two cents, he excused himself from the guys, turning to head for home.

The vivid memory of his nightmarish encounter with the dreaded cu-cui blocked everything from Pelón's mind the next morning. He decided to seek out Santos the first thing. He was waiting at the gate when Mrs. Trigeño came out, dressed for church.

He smiled shyly and watched as she walked down the street before knocking at the door. Santos was drinking a cup of coffee, resuming his seat at the kitchen table when Pelón entered. Explaining his predicament, he confessed his misdeed to the maestro. Pelón sat with bowed head, continuing his confession.

"Maestro, the cu-cui came for me while I slept. It was the most horrible dream I have ever had. It is indeed a monster, so ugly I can't describe it. It said it came for me because I lied to you. I was struggling to wake up but I was trapped by the nightmare and I thought I would die. That is why I came this morning, to confess and get the lie off my conscience. I would not want to have such a nightmare, not ever again."

"You will not have to, Pelón. You must strengthen your will and learn to accept responsibility for everything you do, all of your actions. Then the cu-cui will be like a bothersome puppy you can shoo away. All you have to do is become complete; a perfectly formed man with no vulnerable spots. By the time Gerónimo gets through with you, maybe you will have reached that goal. He will begin your instruction Monday because now you are an official Drop-out and ready for the things he can teach you. Listen, I will give you a chant and send you on your way."

> Pelón, Pelón, Cabeza de Melón,
> cesos de queso con futuro de terrón.
> Te quitamos lo tapado y fue mucho fun,
> Pero eso de ser hombre es facil para none.
> Cuando llega tu tiempo y estas enterrado,
> Sabrás que la risa te mantuvo interesado.
> La vida es dificil, hasta hace llorar,
> fantasía es preciosa, algo que ahorrar.
> Durante los años no dejes de reír,
> Aunque estés triste, con idea de huír.
> Todo que has visto es de un mundo,
> El Señor crió uno, no hay segundo.

> Ahora les hablo a quienes leyeron,
> ojalá les gustó y que lo creyeron.
> El libro fue algo de imaginación,
> porque me gusta gozar, no ser chión.
> Ofrecí mis palabras queriendo su risa,
> comunicarme alegrado es igual que una misa.
> Es modo de decir gracios a Dios,
> me dió audiencia que escuchará mi voz.

> I hoped you liked it and found it funny,
> besides liking to write, I need the money.
> The world can be a bummer, full of sadness,
> that's why I kept it light, including the madness.
> I would like to sit and write you more,
> but things are such I'm an empty store.

I'd sit here typing, really I would,
taxing my mind to create something good.
I know if I sat here and let my thoughts fly,
it would be so outrageous, nobody would buy.
It's poco hard, maintaining a theme,
trying to make it nice like a dream.

And now a word about the language I use,
the use of Spanish and the audience that I lose.
Being Chicano, I talk off-the-wall,
using English and Spanish, but that's not all.
We make up words that defy translation,
corruptions of language causing frustration.
Spanish speakers who talk muy proper,
are shocked to see us loose with a chopper.
Dressed in our culture, we stand at the table,
mixing word-salad as best we are able.
An English word pronounced in Spanish,
a Spanish word pronounced outlandish.
Language is the ingredient and we the cooks,
creating a recipe not found in any books.

That's what this book is, a bowl of stew,
hope the chile isn't too strong for you.
Wanting to sell it and being aware,
taking some trouble and some care.
Brewing it with thought, adding some grease,
knowing that laughter can bring such peace.
I don't know if you'll find it tasty,
give it a chance, don't be too hasty.
Had it been too ethnic, few would buy it,
without manteca, Chicanos wouldn't try it.
I could have written entirely in gavacho,
confining Spanish to easy words like macho.
The Spanish I used I could have translated,
ruining the text in a way I would have hated.

To end this thing, let me just say,
hope it brought laughter to your day.
It was nice to write, lots of fun,
but now I'm sad so the book is done.
What, you wonder, is the matter with him?
I can't hear you laughing and my spirit is dim.
Have no care and don't let it bug you,
it's only temporary, like the flu.
Part of the reason is my mind is a tank,
it fills with joy when there's money in the bank.